PENGUIN

A UNIVERSAL HISTORY OF INIQUITY

JORGE LUIS BORGES was born in Buenos Aires in 1899 and was educated in Europe. One of the most widely acclaimed writers of our time, he published many collections of poems, essays, and short stories before his death in Geneva in June 1986. In 1961 Borges shared the International Publisher's prize with Samuel Beckett. The Ingram Merrill Foundation granted him its Annual Literary Award in 1966 for his "outstanding contribution to literature." In 1971 Columbia University awarded him the first of many degrees of Doctor of Letters, *honoris causa* (eventually the list included both Oxford and Cambridge), that he was to receive from the English-speaking world. In 1971 he also received the fifth biennial Jerusalem Prize and in 1973 was given one of Mexico's most prestigious cultural awards, the Alfonso Reyes Prize. In 1980 he shared with Gerardo Diego the Cervantes Prize, the Spanish world's highest literary accolade. Borges was Director of the Argentine National Library from 1955 until 1973.

ANDREW HURLEY is Professor of English at the University of Puerto Rico in San Juan, where he also teaches in the Translation Program. He has translated over two dozen book-length works of history, poetry, and fiction, including novels by Reinaldo Arenas, Ernesto Sabato, Fernando Arrabal, Gustavo Sainz, and Edgardo Rodríguez Juliá and stories by Ana Lydia Vega, and many shorter works.

JORGE LUIS BORGES

A Universal History
of Iniquity

Translated with an Introduction by
ANDREW HURLEY

PENGUIN BOOKS

PENGUIN BOOKS

Published by the Penguin Group
Penguin Group (USA) Inc., 375 Hudson Street, New York, New York 10014, U.S.A.
Penguin Books Ltd, 80 Strand, London WC2R 0RL, England
Penguin Books Australia Ltd, 250 Camberwell Road, Camberwell, Victoria 3124, Australia
Penguin Books Canada Ltd, 10 Alcorn Avenue, Toronto, Ontario, Canada M4V 3B2
Penguin Books India (P) Ltd, 11 Community Centre, Panchsheel Park, New Delhi – 110 017, India
Penguin Group (NZ), cnr Airborne and Rosedale Roads, Albany, Auckland 1310, New Zealand
Penguin Books (South Africa) (Pty) Ltd, 24 Sturdee Avenue, Rosebank, Johannesburg 2196, South Africa

Penguin Books Ltd, Registered Offices:
80 Strand, London WC2R 0RL, England

This edition first published in Penguin Books (U.K.) 2001
Published in Penguin Books (U.S.A.) 2004

5 7 9 10 8 6 4

Translation and notes copyright © Penguin group (USA) Inc., 1998
Introduction copyright © Andrew Hurley, 2001
All rights reserved

Originally published by Emece Editores, Buenos Aires, as *Historia universal del la infamia*.
This translation by Andrew Hurley first published in the volume, *Collected Fictions*
(Viking Penguin, New York, 1998). Copyright © Maria Kodama, 1998.

CIP data available
ISBN 0 14 24.3789 1

Printed in the United States of America
Set in 11/13.25 pt. PostScript Monotype Columbus

Contents

Introduction

These "exercises in narrative prose," as Borges calls them in his introduction to this delightfully quirky volume, did not begin life under what one might consider the most auspicious of circumstances, for they first appeared as Saturday entertainments in the penny-dreadful vein, complete with illustrations. Over a period of about a year (from mid August 1933 to late June 1934),[1] one or sometimes two of the pieces would appear (on a more or less weekly basis) in the Saturday supplement of the Buenos Aires newspaper *Crítica*, a publication whose usual treatment of the day's news was distinctly sensationalist. And for these particular contributions to its pages, Borges seems to have decided to adopt the same somewhat lurid tone, for his pieces chronicle (and appropriately embellish) the deplorable but fascinating lives of Argentine knife fighters, Wild West gunslingers, gentlemanly Southern scoundrels, pirates, con men, false prophets, evil wizards, and seekers of bloody revenge.

But the curious thing is that these dime-novel entertainments are very much unlike the dozens of other pieces that Borges published in the pages of *Crítica* during his two years with the paper, where he was in fact employed as a kind of torch bearer for "high" literature. The story is this: in 1933 the publisher of

1. For exact publishing details the reader should consult the important bibliographic study *Jorge Luis Borges: Bibliografía completa* by Nicolas Helft (Mexico City/Buenos Aires: Fondo de Cultura Económica, 1997).

Crítica decided that he needed to upgrade his paper's image, and to do that he hit upon bringing out a Sunday cultural supplement to compete with the high-toned literary section (edited by the promising young novelist—and Borges' friend—Eduardo Mallea) that came out with the Sunday edition of *La Nación*, Argentina's leading newspaper. *Crítica*'s new supplement was eventually called the *Revista Multicolor* ("The Multicolored [or perhaps Motley] Review"), and the publisher achieved a kind of coup (and underscored his determination to give his newspaper cultural legitimacy) when he managed to persuade Jorge Luis Borges to edit the literary section and to be a major contributor to the supplement. Nor did Borges disappoint his new employer, for in most of the pieces published under his byline during this period he soberly carried out his cultural mission, offering straightforward and more-than-a-little-edifying book reviews, cultural opinion essays, film reviews, short biographical sketches of leading Latin American, Continental, British, and American writers and poets, pieces that we might today call essays in comparative mythology, etc., and translating poems and brief prose passages from French-, German-, and English-speaking authors. But consider the reader of the *Revista Multicolor*'s pages. It must have been intriguing to say the least, and perhaps even a bit disorienting, to see these fine translations and these sober, conventional, distinctly highbrow literary essays cheek by jowl with the blood-and-guts thrillers of the series so titillatingly titled *A Universal History of Iniquity*—and all written by the same young man. It was as though Borges was having a bit of fun with the *Iniquity* pieces by taking on the colors of his tabloid surroundings, and that was the sort of subtle, witty joke that characterized Borges all his life.

Today, looking back, one of the most striking things we see about Borges' production during the *Revista Multicolor* period is precisely that odd duality of high seriousness and fun. Even in this, his first sustained effort at prose narrative, Borges was already indulging the two sides of himself that critics and readers have so often commented on since: the serious side that was erudite, extraordinarily well-read, insightful, thought-provoking, yet somewhat dry if not downright pedantic; and the playful side that loved a good spoof, relished a subtle joke, delighted in sharing with the reader a sly smile or a conspiratorial wink, and was constantly on the alert for the chance to produce a startling and witty juxtaposition.

And yet that sunny, sportive side had its shadows, for the playful pieces that make up this collection all revolve ineluctably around violence, evil-doing, betrayal—*iniquity*, as the title says. The importance of this motif can hardly be overstressed, for it runs throughout Borges' *oeuvre*. Perhaps because of Borges' fame as a writer of erudite fictions that speculate endlessly on time and history, knowledge, personal identity, "reality" versus the imagination, and the other themes that we all are so familiar with, it has been hard for us readers and critics to "see" the vein of violence and brutality that runs throughout the stories. One after another, though, the stories present scenes of murder (both cold- and hot-blooded), throat slitting, political assassination, political and personal betrayal, mob betrayal (there is no honor among thieves in Borges), armed robbery, knife fights, duels, bloodthirsty revenge, war, bloody conquest and destruction . . . (the list goes on and on). There are no doubt several reasons for the persistence of this motif. For one thing, it is clear that Borges (influenced perhaps by the movies, perhaps by the cult of the knife in old-time Buenos Aires) was fascinated by what might be called the aesthetics of violence; one of the pieces in this volume begins with the "dance" of a knife fight, the "tango" that brings two nattily dressed men together for this abstract, cinematic, and oddly erotic scene of death. For another, there is the element of "realism" in many of Borges' stories. We know—he told us over and over— that he was not "interested" in realism, that it was just one more literary convention, that he could "fake it" whenever he wanted to, and yet there is no doubt that Borges' stories often have a verisimilitude, a definiteness, a specificity of time and place that make them almost documentary chronicles of a moment in time, snapshots of a moment in the history of a city and a country—and that history was a violent one, as Borges also tells us. (On one side, he reminds us, his was a military family; he also reminds us that he had grown up in the neighborhood of Palermo in old Buenos Aires, where knife fights were not simply common, they were the accepted norm.) Associated with this verisimilitude may be a resignation in the face of "the facts," a sense that "life is like that," that violence has been and continued to be the fundamental, perhaps essential, way that humans solved their problems, that it underlay (as we see in "The Duel" in *Brodie's Report*) even the apparently trivial rivalry between two female and decidedly lady-like painters.

A "higher" (and ethically more palatable) reason for the constant motif of violence might be that however much Borges declawed and even glamorized violence by aesthetizing it, he clearly perceived its essential stupidity and brutality ("*bruto*" in Spanish means both bestial and stupid) and, by making violence so central to his stories, was offering a critique of his society—indeed of all humanity, for the stories range over all times and places. This ethical reason for the pervading violence of the stories is often overlooked, especially by those who see Borges as an aloof and mandarin writer disconnected from "social issues," but if we glance at stories such as "*Deutsches Requiem*" in *The Aleph* we see Borges the social critic offering a devastating critique of dehumanized and dehumanizing violence. In a 1933 review (contemporary with the pieces in *History of Iniquity*) of a book entitled *X-Ray of the Pampas*, Borges praised the author, his friend Ezequiel Martínez Estrada, not only for the writing (embodying "a splendid bitterness") but also because Martínez Estrada had helped to invent a new literary genre, neither history nor imaginative narrative nor biography nor economics nor social philosophy-cum-morality à la Carlyle, but something that combined them all: "the pathetic interpretation of the pathetic history of history and even of geography." One might venture to suggest that *A Universal History of Iniquity* is a further work in that genre-bridging genre, and that in it, Borges was following in the footsteps of Oswald Spengler, chronicling the decline into iniquity not just of the West, but, sadly, of the entire human world.

Like all Borges' work, though, the element of "fun," of "entertainment," is present even amid the dark and bloody deeds of the characters of these (invented) biographies. One inspiration for these "exercises in narrative prose" that Borges does not mention in his introduction is Marcel Schwob, author of an eccentric collection of prose pieces titled *Vies Imaginaires*, "Imaginary Lives," which were invented biographies of people about whom not much was known but about whom readers were pretty sure to be curious to know more. (Borges' favorite in the collection was, perhaps not surprisingly, the biography of a pair of notorious murderers.) Borges' collection is even more of a put-on than Schwob's, though, because whereas Schwob clearly informs the reader that his are *imaginary* lives, Borges makes much of the documentary reliability of his biographies, even going so far as to include a "List of Sources" at the end. It was only in a later introduction to a second edition of the book that Borges admitted that far from being historically accurate, these pieces were a "sport" written by a writer who had "*amused* himself [the word is precise] by changing and distorting . . . the stories of other men."

He also amused himself by incorporating the cinema's innovative new techniques of montage, cutting, the close-up, the focus on a telling detail, the creation of "atmosphere." One commentator has called some of the scenes "cartoon-like," and there is little doubt that they do sometimes have the broad, almost burlesque feeling of a comic book in the "True Crime" genre. The cat that perches on Monk Eastman's shoulder and that hangs around Eastman's dead body at the end of the piece—what American reader of a certain age will not be reminded of the bizarre and often grotesque details associated with the gangland characters in the comic strip *Dick Tracy* or the comic books of *Batman* and *Spiderman*? Borges seems to have sensed that that modern kind of morality play—part entertainment, part "true crime," part universal allegory of good and evil, part down-home instructive lesson that "crime does not pay"—was to become our century's most compelling "moral fiction"; the virtuosity of Borges is that he never overplayed his hand, never preached, never moralized, never overtly noted that these were cautionary fictions. He expected the reader to "get it" without his overt help; that respect for the reader is one of the great legacies of Borges, who in this collection foreshadowed all his later techniques and themes, and set the stage for the even more influential fictions that were to come. But *A Universal History of Iniquity* also stands on its own, as a cleverly conceived and beautifully written volume that appealed to readers' taste for thrills, moral uplift, entertainment, and literary "quality," all at the same time. No small feat, and cause for our continued gratitude and delight.

Andrew Hurley
San Juan, Puerto Rico
January 2000

A Universal History
of Iniquity (1935)

I inscribe this book to S.D.—English, innumerable, and an Angel.
Also: I offer her that kernel of myself that I have saved,
somehow—the central heart that deals not in words, traffics not
with dreams, and is untouched by time, by joy, by adversities.

Preface to the First Edition

The exercises in narrative prose that constitute this book were performed from 1933 to 1934. They are derived, I think, from my rereadings of Stevenson and Chesterton, from the first films of von Sternberg, and perhaps from a particular biography of the Argentine poet Evaristo Carriego.* Certain techniques are overused: mismatched lists, abrupt transitions, the reduction of a person's entire life to two or three scenes. (It is this pictorial intention that also governs the story called "Man on Pink Corner.") The stories are not, nor do they attempt to be, psychological.

With regard to the examples of magic that close the book, the only right I can claim to them is that of translator and reader. I sometimes think that good readers are poets as singular, and as awesome, as great authors themselves. No one will deny that the pieces attributed by Valéry to his pluperfect Monsieur Edmond Teste are worth notoriously less than those of his wife and friends.

Reading, meanwhile, is an activity subsequent to writing—more resigned, more civil, more intellectual.

J.L.B.
Buenos Aires
May 27, 1935

Preface to the 1954 Edition

I would define the baroque as that style that deliberately exhausts (or tries to exhaust) its own possibilities, and that borders on self-caricature. In vain did Andrew Lang attempt, in the eighteen-eighties, to imitate Pope's *Odyssey*; it was already a parody, and so defeated the parodist's attempt to exaggerate its tautness. "*Baroco*" was a term used for one of the modes of syllogistic reasoning; the eighteenth century applied it to certain abuses in seventeenth-century architecture and painting. I would venture to say that the baroque is the final stage in all art, when art flaunts and squanders its resources. The baroque is intellectual, and Bernard Shaw has said that all intellectual labor is inherently humorous. This humor is unintentional in the works of Baltasar Gracián* but intentional, even indulged, in the works of John Donne.

The extravagant title of this volume proclaims its baroque nature. Softening its pages would have been equivalent to destroying them; that is why I have preferred, this once, to invoke the biblical words *quod scripsi, scripsi* (John 19:22), and simply reprint them, twenty years later, as they first appeared. They are the irresponsible sport of a shy sort of man who could not bring himself to write short stories, and so amused himself by changing and distorting (sometimes without æsthetic justification) the stories of other men. From these ambiguous exercises, he went on to the arduous composition of a straightforward short story—"Man on Pink Corner"—which he signed with the name of one of his grandfather's grandfathers, Francisco Bustos; the story has had a remarkable, and quite mysterious, success.

In that text, which is written in the accents of the toughs and petty criminals of the Buenos Aires underworld, the reader will note that I have interpolated a number of "cultured" words—*entrails, conversion,* etc. I did this because the tough, the knife fighter, the thug, the type that Buenos Aires calls the *compadre* or *compadrito,* aspires to refinement, or (and this reason excludes the other, but it may be the true one) because *compadres* are individuals and don't always talk like The Compadre, which is a Platonic ideal.

The learned doctors of the Great Vehicle teach us that the essential characteristic of the universe is its emptiness. They are certainly correct with respect to the tiny part of the universe that is this book. Gallows and pirates fill its pages, and that word *iniquity* strikes awe in its title, but under all the storm and lightning, there is nothing. It is all just appearance, a surface of images— which is why readers may, perhaps, enjoy it. The man who made it was a pitiable sort of creature, but he found amusement in writing it; it is to be hoped that some echo of that pleasure may reach its readers.

In the section called *Et cetera* I have added three new pieces.

J.L.B.

The Cruel Redeemer Lazarus Morell

The Remote Cause

In 1517, Fray Bartolomé de las Casas, feeling great pity for the Indians who grew worn and lean in the drudging infernos of the Antillean gold mines, proposed to Emperor Charles V that Negroes be brought to the isles of the Caribbean, so that *they* might grow worn and lean in the drudging infernos of the Antillean gold mines. To that odd variant on the species *philanthropist* we owe an infinitude of things: W. C. Handy's blues; the success achieved in Paris by the Uruguayan attorney-painter Pedro Figari*; the fine runaway-slave prose of the likewise Uruguayan Vicente Rossi*; the mythological stature of Abraham Lincoln; the half-million dead of the War of Secession; the $3.3 billion spent on military pensions; the statue of the imaginary semblance of Antonio (Falucho) Ruiz*; the inclusion of the verb "lynch" in respectable dictionaries; the impetuous King Vidor film *Hallelujah*; the stout bayonet charge of the regiment of "Blacks and Tans" (the color of their skins, not their uniforms) against that famous hill near Montevideo*; the gracefulness of certain elegant young ladies; the black man who killed Martin Fierro; that deplorable rumba *The Peanut-Seller*; the arrested and imprisoned Napoleonism of Toussaint L'Ouverture; the cross and the serpent in Haiti; the blood of goats whose throats are slashed by the *pa-paloi's* machete; the *habanera* that is the mother of the tango; the *candombe*.

And yet another thing: the evil and magnificent existence of the cruel redeemer Lazarus Morell.*

PARADOX

The Place

The Father of Waters, the Mississippi, the grandest river in the world, was the worthy stage for the deeds of that incomparable blackguard. (Alvarez de Pineda discovered this great river, though it was first explored by Hernando de Soto, conqueror of Peru, who whiled away his months in the prison of the Inca Atahualpa teaching his jailer chess. When de Soto died, the river's waters were his grave.)

The Mississippi is a broad-chested river, a dark and infinite brother of the Parana, the Uruguay, the Amazon, and the Orinoco. It is a river of mulatto-hued water; more than four hundred million tons of mud, carried by that water, insult the Gulf of Mexico each year. All that venerable and ancient waste has created a delta where gigantic swamp cypresses grow from the slough of a continent in perpetual dissolution and where labyrinths of clay, dead fish, and swamp reeds push out the borders and extend the peace of their fetid empire. Upstream, Arkansas and Ohio have their bottomlands, too, populated by a jaundiced and hungry-looking race, prone to fevers, whose eyes gleam at the sight of stone and iron, for they know only sand and driftwood and muddy water.

The Men

In the early nineteenth century (the period that interests us) the vast cotton plantations on the riverbanks were worked from sunup to sundown by Negro slaves. They slept in wooden cabins on dirt floors. Apart from the mother-child relationship, kinship was conventional and murky; the slaves had given names, but not always surnames. They did not know how to read. Their soft falsetto voices sang an English of drawn-out vowels. They worked in rows, stooped under the overseer's lash. They would try to escape, and men with full beards would leap astride beautiful horses to hunt them down with baying dogs.

Onto an alluvium of beastlike hopefulness and African fear there had sifted the words of the Scripture; their faith, therefore, was Christian. *Go down, Moses*, they would sing, low and in unison. The Mississippi served them as a magnificent image of the sordid Jordan.

The owners of that hard-worked land and those bands of Negroes were idlers, greedy gentlemen with long hair who lived in wide-fronted mansions that looked out upon the river—their porches always pseudo-Greek with columns made of soft white pine. Good slaves cost a thousand dollars, but they didn't last long. Some were so ungrateful as to sicken and die. A man had to get the most he could out of such uncertain investments. That was why the slaves were in the fields from sunup to sundown; that was why the fields were made to yield up their cotton or tobacco or sugarcane every year. The female soil, worn and haggard from bearing that impatient culture's get, was left barren within a few years, and a formless, clayey desert crept into the plantations.

On broken-down farms, on the outskirts of the cities, in dense fields of sugarcane, and on abject mud flats lived the "poor whites"; they were fishermen, sometime hunters, horse thieves. They would sometimes even beg pieces of stolen food from the Negroes. And yet in their prostration they held one point of pride—their blood, untainted by "the cross of color" and unmixed. Lazarus Morell was one of these men.

The Man

The daguerreotypes printed in American magazines are not actually of Morell. That absence of a genuine likeness of a man as memorable and famous as Morell cannot be coincidental. It is probably safe to assume that Morell refused to sit for the silvered plate—essentially, so as to leave no pointless traces; incidentally, so as to enhance his mystery. . . .We do know, however, that he was not particularly good-looking as a young man and that his close-set eyes and thin lips did not conspire in his favor. The years, as time went on, imparted to him that peculiar majesty that white-haired blackguards, successful (and unpunished) criminals, seem generally to possess. He was a Southern gentleman of the old school, in spite of his impoverished childhood and his shameful life. He was not ignorant of the Scriptures, and he preached with singular conviction. "I once saw Lazarus Morell in the pulpit," wrote the owner of a gambling house in Baton Rouge, "and I heard his edifying words and saw the tears come to his eyes. I knew he was a fornicator, a nigger-stealer, and a murderer in the sight of the Lord, but tears came to my eyes too."

Another testimony to those holy outpourings is provided by Morell himself: "I opened the Bible at random, put my finger on the first verse that came to hand—St. Paul it was—and preached for an hour and twenty minutes. Crenshaw and the boys didn't put that time to bad use, neither, for they rounded up all the folks' horses and made off with 'em. We sold 'em in the state of Arkansas, all but one bay stallion, the most spirited thing you ever laid eyes on, that I kept for myself. Crenshaw had his eye on that horse, too, but I convinced him it warn't the horse for him."

The Method

Horses stolen in one state and sold in another were but the merest digression in Morell's criminal career, but they did prefigure the method that would assure him his place in a Universal History of Iniquity. His method was unique not only because of the *sui generis* circumstances that shaped it, but also because of the depravity it required, its vile manipulation of trust, and its gradual evolution, like the terrifying unfolding of a nightmare. Al Capone and Bugs Moran operate with lavish capital and subservient machine guns in a great city, but their business is vulgar. They fight for a monopoly, and that is the extent of it. . . .In terms of numbers, Morell at one time could command more than a thousand sworn confederates. There were two hundred in the Heads, or General Council, and it was the Heads that gave the orders that the other eight hundred followed. These "strikers," as they were called, ran all the risk. If they stepped out of line, they would be handed over to the law or a rock would be tied to their feet and their bodies would be sunk in the swirling waters of the river. Often, these men were mulattoes. Their wicked mission was this:

In a momentary wealth of gold and silver rings, to inspire respect, they would roam the vast plantations of the South. They would choose some wretched black man and offer him his freedom. They would tell him that if he'd run away from his master and allow them to resell him on another plantation far away, they would give him a share of the money and help him escape a second time. Then, they said, they'd convey him to free soil. . . .Money and freedom—ringing silver dollars and freedom to boot—what greater temptation could they hold out to him? The slave would work up the courage for his first escape.

The river was a natural highway. A canoe, the hold of a riverboat, a barge, a raft as big as the sky with a pilothouse on the bow or with a roof of canvas sheeting . . . the place didn't matter; what mattered was knowing that you were moving, and that you were safe on the unwearying river. . . .They would sell him on another plantation. He would run away again, to the sugarcane fields or the gullies. And it would be then that the fearsome and terrible benefactors (whom he was beginning to distrust by now) would bring up obscure "expenses" and tell him they had to sell him one last time. When he escaped the next time, they told him, they'd give him his percentage of the two sales, and his liberty. The man would let himself be sold, he would work for a while, and then he would risk the dogs and whips and try to escape on his own. He would be brought back bloody, sweaty, desperate, and tired.

The Final Freedom

We have not yet considered the legal aspect of the crime. The Negro would not be put up for sale by Morell's henchmen until his escape had been advertised and a reward offered for his capture. At that point, anybody could lay hold of the slave. Thus, when he was later sold, it was only a breach of trust, not stealing, and it was pointless for the owner to go to law, since he'd never recover his losses.

All this was calculated to leave Morell's mind at ease, but not forever. The Negro could talk; the Negro was capable, out of pure gratitude or misery, of talking. A few drinks of rye whisky in a whorehouse in Cairo, Illinois, where the slave-born son of a bitch went to squander some of those silver dollars burning a hole in his pocket (and that they'd no reason to give him, when it came right down to it), and the cat would be out of the bag. The Abolitionist Party was making things hot in the North during this time—a mob of dangerous madmen who denied a man's right to his own property, preached the freeing of the blacks, and incited the slaves to rebellion. Morell was not about to let himself be confused with those anarchists. He was no Yankee, he was a Southerner, a white man, the son and grandson of white men, and he hoped someday to retire from his business and be a gentleman and possess his own league upon league of cotton fields and his own bowbacked rows of slaves. With his experience, he was not a man to take pointless risks.

The runaway expected his freedom. Therefore, the nebulous mulattoes of Lazarus Morell would give a sign (which might have been no more than a wink) and the runaway would be freed from sight, hearing, touch, daylight, iniquity, time, benefactors, mercy, air, dogs, the universe, hope, sweat—and from himself. A bullet, a low thrust with a blade, a knock on the head, and the turtles and catfish of the Mississippi would be left to keep the secret among themselves.

The Catastrophe

Manned by trustworthy fellows, the business was bound to prosper. By early 1834, some seventy Negro slaves had been "emancipated" by Morell, and others were ready to follow their fortunate forerunners. The zone of operations was larger now, and new members had to be admitted to the gang. Among those who took the oath, there was one young man, Virgil Stewart, from Arkansas, who very soon distinguished himself by his cruelty. This boy was the nephew of a gentleman who had lost a great number of slaves. In August of 1834, he broke his vow and denounced Morell and the others. Morell's house in New Orleans was surrounded by the authorities, but Morell somehow (owing to some oversight—or a bribe in the right quarters) managed to escape.

Three days passed. Morell hid for that period in an old house with vine-covered courtyards and statues, on Toulouse Street. Apparently he had almost nothing to eat and spent his days roaming barefoot through the large, dark rooms, smoking a thoughtful cheroot. Through a slave in the house, he sent two letters to Natchez and another to Red River. On the fourth day, three men entered the house; they sat talking things over with Morell until almost daybreak. On the fifth day, Morell got out of bed at nightfall, borrowed a razor, and carefully shaved off his beard. He then dressed and left the house. Slowly and calmly he made his way through the northern outskirts of the city. When he reached open country, out in the bottomlands of the Mississippi, he breathed easier.

His plan was one of drunken courage. He proposed to exploit the last men that still owed him respect: the accommodating Negroes of the Southland themselves. These men had seen their comrades run away, and had not seen them brought back. They thought, therefore, that they'd found freedom. Morell's plan called for a general uprising of the Negroes, the capture and sack of New Orleans, and the occupation of the territory. A pitiless and depraved man, and now almost undone by treachery, Morell planned a response of continental proportions—a response in which criminality would become redemptive, and historic. To that end, he headed for Natchez, where his strength ran deeper. I reproduce his own narration of that journey:

"I walked four days," he reported, "and no opportunity offered for me to get a horse. The fifth day, I had . . . stopped at a creek to get some water and rest a while. While I was sitting on a log, looking down the road the way that I had come, a man came in sight riding on a good-looking horse. The very moment I saw him, I was determined to have his horse. . . .I arose and drew an elegant rifle pistol on him and ordered him to dismount. He did so, and I took his horse by the bridle and pointed down the creek, and ordered him to walk before me. He went a few hundred yards and stopped. I . . . made him undress himself, all to his shirt and drawers, and ordered him to turn his back to me. He said, 'If you are determined to kill me, let me have time to pray before I die.' I told him I had no time to hear him pray. He turned around and dropped on his knees, and I shot him through the back of the head. I ripped open his belly and took out his entrails, and sunk him in the creek. I then searched his pockets, and found four hundred dollars and thirty-seven cents, and a number of papers that I did not take time to examine. I sunk the pocket-book and papers·and his hat, in the creek. His boots were bran-new, and fitted me genteelly; and I put them on and sunk my old shoes in the creek. . . .

"I mounted as fine a horse as ever I straddled, and directed my course for Natchez."*

The Interruption

Morell leading uprisings of Negroes that dreamed of hanging him . . . Morell hanged by armies of Negroes that he had dreamed of leading . . . it pains me to admit that the history of the Mississippi did not seize upon those rich opportunities. Nor, contrary to all poetic justice (and poetic symmetry), did the river of his crimes become his tomb. On the 2nd of January, 1835, Lazarus Morell died of pulmonary congestion in the hospital at Natchez, where he'd been admitted under the name Silas Buckley. Another man in the ward recognized him. On that day, and on the 4th of January, slaves on scattered plantations attempted to revolt, but they were put down with no great loss of blood.

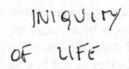

The Improbable Impostor
Tom Castro

I give him that name because it was by that name he was known
(in 1850 or thereabouts) on the streets and in the houses of
Talcahuano, Santiago de Chile, and Valparaíso, and it seems only
fair that he take it again, now that he has returned to those
lands—even if only as a ghost, or a Saturday-night amusement.[1]
The birth register in Wapping calls him Arthur Orton, and gives
the date of his birth as June 7, 1834. We know that he was the
son of a butcher, that his childhood was spent in the gray meanness
of the London slums, and that he harkened to the call of the sea.
That story is not an uncommon one; "running away to sea" was
the traditional English way to break with parental authority—
the heroic ritual of initiation. Geography recommended such a
course, as did the Scriptures themselves: "*They that go down to the
sea in ships, that do business in great waters; these see the works of the
Lord, and his wonders in the deep*" (Psalms 107:23–24). Orton fled
his deplorable, dingy-pink-colored suburb and went down to the
sea in a ship; with ingrained disappointment he regarded the
Southern Cross, and he jumped ship at Valparaíso. He was a
gentle idiot. Though by all logic he could (and should) have
starved to death, his muddle-headed joviality, his permanent grin,
and his infinite docility earned him the favor of a certain family
named Castro, whose patronym he took ever after as his own. No

---

[1]. I have chosen this metaphor in order to remind the reader that these vile
biographies appeared in the Saturday supplement of an evening newspaper.

16

traces of his stay in South America remain, but we know that his gratitude never flagged: in 1861 he turned up in Australia, still bearing the name Tom Castro.

In Sydney he made the acquaintance of a man named Ebenezer Bogle, a Negro servant. Bogle, though not handsome, had that reposeful and monumental air, that look of well-engineered solidity, often possessed by a black man of a certain age, a certain corporeal substance, a certain authority. Bogle had another quality, as well—though some textbooks in anthropology deny the attribute to his race: he was possessed of genius. (We shall see the proof of that soon enough.) He was a temperate, decent man, the ancient African appetites in him corrected by the customs and excesses of Calvinism. Aside from the visitations from his god (which we shall describe below), he was normal in every way; his only eccentricity was a deep-seated and shamefaced fear that made him hesitate at street corners and at crossings, survey east, west, north, and south, and try to outguess the violent vehicle that he was certain would end his days.

Orton came upon his future friend one afternoon as Bogle was standing on a run-down corner in Sydney trying to screw up the courage to face his imagined death. After watching him for several minutes, Orton offered him his arm, and the two astounded men crossed the inoffensive street. Out of that now-bygone evening a protectorate was forged: the monumental, unsure Negro over the obese Wapping simpleton. In September of 1865, the two men read a heartbreaking piece of news in the local paper.

The Adored One Deceased

In the waning days of April, 1854 (as Orton was inspiring the effusions of Chilean hospitality, which was as welcoming as that country's patios), there had sunk in the waters of the Atlantic a steamship christened the *Mermaid*, bound from Rio de Janeiro to

Liverpool. Among the drowned had been one Roger Charles Tichborne, an English military officer brought up in France, and the firstborn son of one of England's leading Catholic families. However improbable it may seem, the death of this Frenchified young man (a young man who had spoken English with the most cultured of Parisian accents and who had inspired the unparalleled envy that can only be aroused by French intelligence, grace, and affectation) was an event of supreme importance in the destiny of Arthur Orton, who had never so much as laid eyes on him. Lady Tichborne, Roger's horrified mother, refused to believe the reports of his death. She published heartrending advertisements in all the major newspapers, and one of those advertisements fell into the soft, funereal hands of Ebenezer Bogle, who conceived a brilliant plan.

The Virtues of Unlikeness

Tichborne had been a slim, genteel young man with a reserved and somewhat self-absorbed air. He had sharp features, straight black hair, tawny skin, sparkling eyes, and an irritatingly precise way of speaking. Orton was an irrepressible rustic, a "yokel," with a vast belly, features of infinite vagueness, fair and freckled skin, wavy light-brown hair, sleepy eyes, and no, or irrelevant, conversation. Bogle decided that it was Orton's duty to take the first steamer for Europe and realize Lady Tichborne's hope that her son had not perished—by declaring himself to be that son. The plan had an irrational genius to it. Let me give a simple example: If an impostor had wanted to pass himself off as the emperor of Germany and king of Prussia in 1914, the first thing he'd have done would be fake the upturned mustaches, the lifeless arm, the authoritarian scowl, the gray cape, the illustrious and much-decorated chest, and the high helmet. Bogle was more subtle: he would have brought forth a smooth-faced Kaiser with no military traits, no proud eagles whatsoever, and a left arm in unquestionable health. We have no need of the metaphor; we know for a fact that Bogle produced a fat, flabby Tichborne with the sweet smile of an idiot, light-brown hair, and a thoroughgoing ignorance of French. Bogle knew that a perfect facsimile of the beloved Roger Charles Tichborne was impossible to find; he knew as well that any similarities he might achieve would only underscore certain inevitable differences. He therefore gave up the notion of likeness altogether. He sensed that the vast ineptitude of his pretense would be a convincing proof that this was no fraud, for no fraud would ever have so flagrantly flaunted features that might so easily have convinced. We should also not overlook the all-powerful collaboration of time: the vicissitudes of fortune, and fourteen years of antipodean life, can change a man.

Another essential argument in favor of Bogle's plan: Lady Tichborne's repeated and irrational advertisements showed that she was certain that Roger Charles had not died, and that she would will herself to recognize him when he came.

The Meeting

Tom Castro, ever accommodating, wrote to Lady Tichborne. In order to prove his identity, he invoked the irrefutable proof of the two moles near his left nipple and that painful and therefore unforgettable episode from his childhood when a swarm of bees had attacked him. The letter was brief and, in the image of Bogle and Tom Castro, free of any scruples as to the way words ought to be spelled. In her majestic solitude in her *hôtel particulier* in Paris, Lady Tichborne read and reread the letter through happy tears, and in a few days she had recaptured the recollections her son had invoked.

On January 16, 1867, Roger Charles Tichborne called upon his mother. His respectful servant, Ebenezer Bogle, preceded him. It was a winter day of bright sunshine; Lady Tichborne's tired eyes were veiled with tears. The black man threw the windows open. The light served as a mask; the mother recognized the prodigal and opened her arms to him. Now that she had him in the flesh, she might do without his diary and the letters he had written her from Brazil—the treasured reflections of the son which had fed her loneliness through those fourteen melancholy years. She returned them to him proudly; not one was missing.

Bogle smiled discreetly; now he could research the gentle ghost of Roger Charles.   LIFE / LETTERS

Ad Majorem Dei Gloriam

That joyous recognition, which seems to obey the tradition of classical tragedy, should be the crown of this story, leaving happiness assured (or at least more than possible) for the three persons of the tale—the true mother, the apocryphal and obliging son, and the conspirator repaid for the providential apotheosis of his industry. But Fate (for such is the name that we give the infinite and unceasing operation of thousands of intertwined causes) would not have it. Lady Tichborne died in 1870, and the family brought charges against Arthur Orton for impersonation and usurpation of their dead kinsman's estate. As they themselves were afflicted with neither tears nor loneliness (though the same cannot be said of greed), they had never believed in the obese and almost illiterate lost son who had so inopportunely reappeared from Australia.

Orton's claim was supported by the innumerable creditors who had decided that he was Tichborne; they wanted their bills paid. He also drew upon the friendship of the old family solicitor, Edward Hopkins, and that of an antiquary named Francis J. Baigent. But this, though much, was not enough. Bogle believed that if they were to win this round, a groundswell of public support was wanted. He called for his top hat and his black umbrella and he went out for a walk through the decorous streets of London, in search of inspiration. It was just evening; Bogle wandered about until a honey-colored moon was mirrored in the rectangular waters of the public fountains. And then he was visited by his god. Bogle whistled for a cab and had himself driven to the flat of the antiquary Baigent. Baigent sent a long letter to the *Times*, denouncing this "Tichborne claimant" as a brazen hoax. The letter was signed by Father Goudron, of the Society of Jesus. Other, equally papist, denunciations followed. The effect was immediate: the right sort of person could not fail to see that Sir Roger Charles Tichborne was the target of a despicable Jesuit plot.

The Coach

The trial lasted one hundred ninety days. Some hundred witnesses swore that the accused was Roger Charles Tichborne—among them, four comrades-at-arms from the 6th Dragoons. Orton's supporters steadfastly maintained that he was no impostor—had he been, they pointed out, he would surely have attempted to copy the juvenile portraits of his model. And besides, Lady Tichborne had recognized and accepted him; clearly, in such matters, a mother does not err. All was going well, then—more or less—until an old sweetheart of Orton's was called to testify. Not a muscle of Bogle's face twitched at that perfidious maneuver by the "family"; he called for his black umbrella and his top hat and he went out into the decorous streets of London to seek a third inspiration. We shall never know whether he found it. Shortly before he came to Primrose Hill, he was struck by that terrible vehicle that had been pursuing him through all these years. Bogle saw it coming and managed to cry out, but he could not manage to save himself. He was thrown violently against the paving stones. The hack's dizzying hooves cracked his skull open.

The Specter

Tom Castro was Tichborne's ghost, but a poor sort of ghost, inhabited by the *daemon* Bogle. When he was told that Bogle had been killed, he simply collapsed. He continued to tell his lies, but with very little enthusiasm and a great deal of self-contradiction. It was easy to foresee the end.

On the 27th of February, 1874, Arthur Orton (alias Tom Castro) was sentenced to fourteen years' penal servitude. In gaol he made himself beloved by all; it was his lifework. His exemplary behavior won him a reduction of four years off his sentence. When that final hospitality—the prison's—ran out on him, he wandered the towns and villages of the United Kingdom, giving lectures in which he would alternately declare his innocence and confess his guilt. His modesty and his desire to please remained with him always; many nights he would begin by defending himself and wind up admitting all, depending upon the inclinations of his audience.

On the 2nd of April, 1898, he died.

The Widow Ching—Pirate

The author who uses the phrase "female corsairs" runs the risk of calling up an awkward image—that of the now-faded Spanish operetta with its theories of obvious servant girls playing the part of choreographed pirates on noticeably cardboard seas. And yet there *have* been cases of female pirates—women skilled in the art of sailing, the governance of barbarous crews, the pursuit and looting of majestic ships on the high seas. One such woman was Mary Read, who was quoted once as saying that the profession of piracy wasn't for just anybody, and if you were going to practice it with dignity, you had to be a man of courage, like herself. In the crude beginnings of her career, when she was not yet the captain of her own ship, a young man she fancied was insulted by the ship's bully. Mary herself picked a quarrel with the bully and fought him hand to hand, in the old way of the isles of the Caribbean: the long, narrow, and undependable breechloader in her left hand, the trusty saber in her right. The pistol failed her, but the saber acquitted itself admirably. . . .In 1720 the bold career of Mary Read was interrupted by a Spanish gallows, in Santiago de la Vega, on the island of Jamaica.

Another female pirate of those waters was Anne Bonney, a magnificent Irishwoman of high breasts and fiery hair who risked her life more than once in boarding ships. She stood on the deck with Mary Read, and then with her on the scaffold. Her lover, Captain John Rackham, met his own noose at that same hanging. Anne, contemptuous, emerged with that harsh variant on Aixa's rebuke to Boabdil*: "If you'd fought like a man, you needn't have been hang'd like a dog."

Another woman pirate, but a more daring and long-lived one, plied the waters of far Asia, from the Yellow Sea to the rivers on the borders of Annam. I am speaking of the doughty widow Ching.

The Years of Apprenticeship

In 1797 the shareholders in the many pirate ships of the Yellow Sea formed a consortium, and they chose one Captain Ching, a just (though strict) man, tested under fire, to be the admiral of their new fleet. Ching was so harsh and exemplary in his sacking of the coasts that the terrified residents implored the emperor with gifts and tears to send them aid. Nor did their pitiable request fall upon deaf ears: they were ordered to set fire to their villages, abandon their fisheries, move inland, and learn the unknown science of agriculture. They did all this; and so, finding only deserted coastlines, the frustrated invaders were forced into way-laying ships—a depredation far more unwelcome than raids on the coasts, for it seriously threatened trade. Once again, the imperial government responded decisively: it ordered the former fishermen to abandon their plows and oxen and return to their oars and nets. At this, the peasants, recalling their former terrors, balked, so the authorities determined upon another course: they would make Admiral Ching the Master of the Royal Stables. Ching was willing to accept the buy-off. The stockholders, how-ever, learned of the decision in the nick of time, and their righteous indignation took the form of a plate of rice served up with poisoned greens. The delicacy proved fatal; the soul of the former admiral and newly appointed Master of the Royal Stables was delivered up to the deities of the sea. His widow, transfigured by the double treachery, called the pirates together, explained the complex case, and exhorted them to spurn both the emperor's deceitful clemency and odious employment in the service of the shareholders with a bent for poison. She proposed what might be called freelance piracy. She also proposed that they cast votes for a new admiral, and she herself was elected. She was a sapling-thin woman of sleepy eyes and caries-riddled smile. Her oiled black hair shone brighter than her eyes.

Under Mrs. Ching's calm command, the ships launched forth into danger and onto the high seas.

The Command

Thirteen years of methodical adventuring ensued. The fleet was composed of six squadrons, each under its own banner—red, yellow, green, black, purple—and one, the admiral's own, with the emblem of a serpent. The commanders of the squadrons had such names as Bird and Stone, Scourge of the Eastern Sea, Jewel of the Whole Crew, Wave of Many Fishes, and High Sun. The rules of the fleet, composed by the widow Ching herself, were unappealable and severe, and their measured, laconic style was devoid of those withered flowers of rhetoric that lend a ridiculous sort of majesty to the usual official pronouncements of the Chinese (an alarming example of which, we shall encounter shortly). Here are some of the articles of the fleet's law:

Not the least thing shall be taken privately from the stolen and plundered goods. All shall be registered, and the pirate receive for himself out of ten parts, only two: eight parts belong to the storehouse, called the general fund; taking anything out of this general fund without permission shall be death.

If any man goes privately on shore, or what is called transgressing the bars, he shall be taken and his ears perforated in the presence of the whole fleet; repeating the same, he shall suffer death.

No person shall debauch at his pleasure captive women taken in the villages and open spaces, and brought on board a ship; he must first request the ship's purser for permission and then go aside in the ship's hold. To use violence against any woman without permission of the purser shall be punished by death. *

Reports brought back by prisoners state that the mess on the pirate ships consisted mainly of hardtack, fattened rats, and cooked rice; on days of combat, the crew would mix gunpowder with their liquor. Marked cards and loaded dice, drinking and fan-tan, the visions of the opium pipe and little lamp filled idle hours. Two swords, simultaneously employed, were the weapon of choice. Before a boarding, the pirates would sprinkle their cheeks and bodies with garlic water, a sure charm against injury by fire breathed from muzzles.

The crew of a ship traveled with their women, the captain with his harem—which might consist of five or six women, and be renewed with each successive victory.

The Young Emperor Chia-Ch'ing Speaks

In June or July of 1809, an imperial decree was issued, from which I translate the first paragraph and the last. Many people criticized its style:

Miserable and injurious men, men who stamp upon bread, men who ignore the outcry of tax collectors and orphans, men whose smallclothes bear the figure of the phoenix and the dragon, men who deny the truth of printed books, men who let their tears flow facing North—such men disturb the happiness of our rivers and the erstwhile trustworthiness of our seas. Day and night, their frail and crippled ships defy the tempest. Their object is not a benevolent one: they are not, and never have been, the seaman's bosom friend. Far from lending aid, they fall upon him with ferocity, and make him an unwilling guest of ruin, mutilation, and even death. Thus these men violate the natural laws of the Universe, and their offenses make rivers overflow their banks and flood the plains, sons turn against their fathers, the principles of wetness and dryness exchange places. . . .

Therefore, I commend thee to the punishment of these crimes, Admiral Kwo-Lang. Never forget—clemency is the Emperor's to give; the Emperor's subject would be presumptuous in granting it. Be cruel, be just, be obeyed, be victorious.

The incidental reference to the "crippled ships" was, of course, a lie; its purpose was to raise the courage of Kwo-Lang's expedition. Ninety days later, the forces of the widow Ching engaged the empire's. Almost a thousand ships did battle from sunup to sundown. A mixed chorus of bells, drums, cannon bursts, curses, gongs, and prophecies accompanied the action. The empire's fleet was destroyed; Admiral Kwo-Lang found occasion to exercise neither the mercy forbidden him nor the cruelty to which he was exhorted. He himself performed a ritual which our own defeated generals choose not to observe—he committed suicide.

The Terrified Coastlines and Riverbanks

Then the six hundred junks of war and the haughty widow's forty thousand victorious pirates sailed into the mouth of the Zhu-Jiang River, sowing fire and appalling celebrations and orphans left and right. Entire villages were razed. In one of them, the prisoners numbered more than a thousand. One hundred twenty women who fled to the pathless refuge of the nearby stands of reeds or the paddy fields were betrayed by the crying of a baby, and sold into slavery in Macao. Though distant, the pathetic tears and cries of mourning from these depredations came to the notice of Chia-Ch'ing, the Son of Heaven. Certain historians have allowed themselves to believe that the news of the ravaging of his people caused the emperor less pain than did the defeat of his punitive expedition. Be that as it may, the emperor organized a second expedition, terrible in banners, sailors, soldiers, implements of war, provisions, soothsayers and astrologers. This time, the force was under the command of Admiral Ting-kwei-heu. The heavy swarm of ships sailed into the mouth of the Zhu-Jiang to cut off the pirate fleet. The widow rushed to prepare for battle. She knew it would be hard, very hard, almost desperate; her men, after many nights (and even months) of pillaging and idleness, had grown soft. But the battle did not begin. The sun peacefully rose and without haste set again into the quivering reeds. The men and the arms watched, and waited. The noontimes were more powerful than they, and the siestas were infinite.

The Dragon and the Vixen

And yet each evening, lazy flocks of weightless dragons rose high into the sky above the ships of the imperial fleet and hovered delicately above the water, above the enemy decks. These cometlike kites were airy constructions of rice paper and reed, and each silvery or red body bore the identical characters. The widow anxiously studied that regular flight of meteors, and in it read the confused and slowly told fable of a dragon that had always watched over a vixen, in spite of the vixen's long ingratitude and constant crimes. The moon grew thin in the sky, and still the figures of rice paper and reed wrote the same story each evening, with almost imperceptible variations. The widow was troubled, and she brooded. When the moon grew fat in the sky and in the red-tinged water, the story seemed to be reaching its end. No one could predict whether infinite pardon or infinite punishment was to be let fall upon the vixen, yet the inevitable end, whichever it might be, was surely approaching. The widow understood. She threw her two swords into the river, knelt in the bottom of a boat, and ordered that she be taken to the flagship of the emperor's fleet.

It was evening; the sky was filled with dragons—this time, yellow ones. The widow murmured a single sentence, "The vixen seeks the dragon's wing," as she stepped aboard the ship.

The Apotheosis

The chroniclers report that the vixen obtained her pardon, and that she dedicated her slow old age to opium smuggling. She was no longer "The Widow"; she assumed a name that might be translated "The Luster of True Instruction."

From this period (writes a historian) ships began to pass and repass in tranquillity. All became quiet on the rivers and tranquil on the four seas. People lived in peace and plenty. Men sold their arms and bought oxen to plough their fields. They buried sacrifices, said prayers on the tops of hills, and rejoiced themselves by singing behind screens during the day-time. *

Monk Eastman, Purveyor
of Iniquities

The Toughs of One America

Whether profiled against a backdrop of blue-painted walls or of the sky itself, two toughs sheathed in grave black clothing dance, in boots with high-stacked heels, a solemn dance—the tango of evenly matched knives—until suddenly, a carnation drops from behind an ear, for a knife has plunged into a man, whose horizontal dying brings the dance without music to its end. Resigned,* the other man adjusts his hat and devotes the years of his old age to telling the story of that clean-fought duel. That, to the least and last detail, is the story of the Argentine underworld. The story of the thugs and ruffians of New York has much more speed, and much less grace.

The Toughs of Another

The story of the New York gangs (told in 1928 by Herbert Asbury in a decorous volume of some four hundred octavo pages) possesses all the confusion and cruelty of barbarian cosmologies, and much of their gigantism and ineptitude. The chaotic story takes place in the cellars of old breweries turned into Negro tenements, in a seedy, three-story New York City filled with gangs of thugs like the Swamp Angels, who would swarm out of labyrinthine sewers on marauding expeditions; gangs of cutthroats like the Daybreak Boys, who recruited precocious murderers of ten and eleven years old; brazen, solitary giants like the Plug Uglies, whose stiff bowler hats stuffed with wool and whose vast shirttails blowing in the wind of the slums might provoke a passerby's improbable smile, but who carried huge bludgeons in their right hands and long, narrow pistols; and gangs of street toughs like the Dead Rabbit gang, who entered into battle under the banner of their mascot impaled upon a pike. Its characters were men like Dandy Johnny Dolan, famed for his brilliantined forelock, the monkey-headed walking sticks he carried, and the delicate copper pick he wore on his thumb to gouge out his enemies' eyes; men like Kit Burns, who was known to bite the head off live rats; and men like blind Danny Lyons, a towheaded kid with huge dead eyes who pimped for three whores that proudly walked the streets for him. There were rows of red-light houses, such as those run by the seven New England sisters that gave all the profits from their Christmas Eves to charity; rat fights and dog fights; Chinese gambling dens; women like the oft-widowed Red Norah, who was squired about and loved by every leader of the famous Gophers, or Lizzy the Dove, who put on black when Danny Lyons was murdered and got her throat cut for it by Gentle Maggie, who took exception to Lizzy's old affair with the dead blind man; riots such as that of the savage week of 1863 when a hundred buildings were burned to the ground and the entire city was lucky to escape the flames; street brawls when a man would be as lost as if he'd drowned, for he'd be stomped to death; and thieves and horse poisoners like Yoske Nigger. The most famous hero of the story of the New York City underworld is Edward Delaney, alias William Delaney, alias Joseph Marvin, alias Joseph Morris—alias Monk Eastman, the leader of a gang of twelve hundred men.

The Hero

Those shifting "dodges" (as tedious as a game of masks in which one can never be certain who is who) fail to include the man's true name—if we allow ourselves to believe that there is such a thing as "a man's true name." The fact is, the name given in the Records Division of the Williamsburg section of Brooklyn is Edward Ostermann, later Americanized to Eastman. Odd—this brawling and tempestuous hoodlum was Jewish. He was the son of the owner of a restaurant that billed itself as kosher, where men with rabbinical beards might trustingly consume the bled and thrice-clean meat of calves whose throats had been slit with righteousness. With his father's backing, in 1892, at the age of nineteen, he opened a pet shop specializing in birds. Observing the life of animals, studying their small decisions, their inscrutable innocence, was a passion that accompanied Monk Eastman to the end. In later times of magnificence, when he scorned the cigars of the freckled sachems of Tammany Hall and pulled up to the finest whorehouses in one of New York's first automobiles (a machine that looked like the by-blow of a Venetian gondola), he opened a second establishment, this one a front, that was home to a hundred purebred cats and more than four hundred pigeons— none of which were for sale at any price. He loved every one of the creatures, and would often stroll through the streets of the neighborhood with one purring cat on his arm and others trailing along ambitiously in his wake.

He was a battered and monumental man. He had a short, bull neck, an unassailable chest, the long arms of a boxer, a broken nose; his face, though legended with scars, was less imposing than his body. He was bowlegged, like a jockey or a sailor. He might go shirtless or collarless, and often went without a coat, but he was never seen without a narrow-brimmed derby atop his enormous head. He is still remembered. Physically, the conventional gunman of the moving pictures is modeled after *him*, not the flabby and epicene Capone. It has been said that Louis Wolheim was used in Hollywood films because his features reminded people of the deplorable Monk Eastman. . . .Eastman would leave his house to inspect his gangster empire with a blue-feathered pigeon perched on his shoulder, like a bull with a heron on its hump.

In 1894 there were many dance halls in New York City; Eastman was a bouncer in one of them. Legend has it that the manager wouldn't talk to him about the job, so Monk showed his qualifications by roundly demolishing the two gorillas that stood in the way of his employment. He held the job until 1899—feared, and single-handed.

For every obstreperous customer he subdued, he would cut a notch in the bludgeon he carried. One night, a shining bald spot leaning over a beer caught his eye, and Eastman laid the man's scalp open with a tremendous blow. "I had forty-nine nicks in me stick, an' I wanted to make it an even fifty!" Eastman later explained.

Ruling the Roost

From 1899 onward, Eastman was not just famous, he was the ward boss of an important electoral district in the city, and he collected large payoffs from the red-light houses, stuss games, streetwalkers, pickpockets, loft burglars, and footpads of that sordid fiefdom. The Party would contract him when some mischief needed doing, and private individuals would come to him too. These are the fees he would charge for a job:

Ear chawed off	$15.
Leg broke	19.
Shot in leg	25.
Stab	25.
Doing the big job	100. and up

Sometimes, to keep his hand in, Eastman would do the job personally.

A territorial dispute as subtle and ill humored as those forestalled by international law brought him up against Paul Kelly, the famous leader of another gang. The boundary line had been established by bullets and border patrol skirmishes. Eastman crossed the line late one night and was set upon by five of Kelly's men. With his blackjack and those lightning-quick simian arms of his, he managed to knock down three of them, but he was shot twice in the stomach and left for dead. He stuck his thumb and forefinger in the hot wounds and staggered to the hospital. Life, high fever, and death contended over Monk Eastman for several weeks, but his lips would not divulge the names of his assailants. By the time he left the hospital, the war was in full swing. There was one shoot-out after another, and this went on for two years, until the 19th of August, 1903.

The Battle of Rivington Street

A hundred or more heroes, none quite resembling the mug shot probably fading at that very moment in the mug books; a hundred heroes reeking of cigar smoke and alcohol; a hundred heroes in straw boaters with bright-colored bands; a hundred heroes, all suffering to a greater or lesser degree from shameful diseases, tooth decay, respiratory ailments, or problems with their kidneys; a hundred heroes as insignificant or splendid as those of Troy or Junín*—those were the men that fought that black deed of arms in the shadow of the elevated train. The cause of it was a raid that Kelly's "enforcers" had made on a stuss game under Monk Eastman's protection. One of Kelly's men was killed, and the subsequent shoot-out grew into a battle of uncountable revolvers. From behind the tall pillars of the El, silent men with clean-shaven chins blazed away at one another; soon, they were the center of a horrified circle of hired hacks carrying impatient reinforcements clutching Colt artillery. What were the protagonists in the battle feeling? First, I believe, the brutal conviction that the senseless, deafening noise of a hundred revolvers was going to annihilate them instantly; second, I believe, the no less erroneous certainty that if the initial volley didn't get them, they were invulnerable. Speculation notwithstanding, behind their parapets of iron and the night, they battled furiously. Twice the police tried to intervene, and twice they were repelled. At the first light of dawn, the battle died away, as though it were spectral, or obscene. Under the tall arches raised by engineers, what remained were seven men gravely wounded, four men dead, and one lifeless pigeon.

The Crackle of Gunfire

The ward politicians for whom Monk Eastman worked had always publicly denied that such gangs existed, or had clarified that they were merely social clubs. The indiscreet battle on Rivington Street alarmed them. They called in Eastman and Kelly and impressed upon them the need to declare a truce. Kelly, who recognized that politicians were better than all the Colts ever made when it came to dissuading the police from their duty, immediately saw the light; Eastman, with the arrogance of his great stupid body, was spoiling for more grudge fights and more bullets. At first, he wouldn't hear of a truce, but the politicos threatened him with prison. Finally the two illustrious thugs were brought together in a downtown dive; each man had a cigar clenched in his teeth, his right hand on his gun, and his watchful swarm of armed bodyguards hovering nearby. They came to a very American sort of decision—they would let the dispute be settled by a boxing match. Kelly was a skilled boxer. The match took place in an old barn, and it was stranger than fiction. One hundred forty spectators watched—toughs in cocked derby hats and women in

"Mikado tuck-ups," the high-piled, delicate hairdos of the day. The fight lasted two hours, and it ended in utter exhaustion. Within a week, gunshots were crackling again. Monk was arrested, for the umpteenth time. The police, relieved, derived great amusement from his arrest; the judge prophesied for him, quite correctly, ten years in prison.

Eastman vs. Germany

When the still-perplexed Monk Eastman got out of Sing Sing, the twelve hundred toughs in his gang had scattered. He couldn't manage to round them up again, so he resigned himself to working on his own. On the 8th of September, 1917, he was arrested for fighting and charged with disturbing the peace. On the 9th, he felt like he needed another sort of fight, and he enlisted in the Army.

We know several details of his service. We know that he was fervently opposed to the taking of prisoners, and that once (with just his rifle butt) he prevented that deplorable practice. We know that once he escaped from the hospital and made his way back to the trenches. We know that he distinguished himself in the conflicts near Montfaucon. We know that afterward he was heard to say that in his opinion there were lots of dance halls in the Bowery that were tougher than that so-called "Great War" of theirs.

The Mysterious Logical End

On the 25th of December, 1920, Monk Eastman's body was found on one of New York's downtown streets. He had been shot five times. A common alley cat, blissfully ignorant of death, was pacing, a bit perplexedly, about the body.*

The Disinterested Killer
Bill Harrigan

The image of the lands of Arizona, before any other image—
Arizona and New Mexico. A landscape dazzlingly underlain with
gold and silver, a windblown, dizzying landscape of monumental
mesas and delicate colorations, with the white glare of a skeleton
stripped bare by hawks and buzzards. Within this landscape,
another image—the image of Billy the Kid, the rider sitting firm
upon his horse, the young man of loud shots that stun the desert,
the shooter of invisible bullets that kill at a distance, like a magic
spell.

The arid, glaring desert veined with minerals. The almost-child
who died at the age of twenty-one owing a debt to human justice
for the deaths of twenty-one men—"not counting Mexicans."

The Larval State

In 1859, the man who in terror and glory would be known as
Billy the Kid was born in a basement lodging in New York City.
They say it was a worn-out Irish womb that bore him, but that
he was brought up among Negroes. In that chaos of kinky hair
and rank sweat, he enjoyed the primacy lent by freckles and a
shock of auburn hair. He practiced the arrogance of being white;
he was also scrawny, quick-tempered, and foulmouthed. By the
age of twelve he was one of the Swamp Angels, a gang of deities
whose lair was the sewers of the city. On nights that smelled of

burned fog they would swarm out of that fetid labyrinth, follow the trail of some German sailor, bring him down with a blow to his head, strip him of all he owned, even his underwear, and return once more to that other scum. They were under the command of a white-haired Negro named Jonas, a member of the Gas House gang and a man famed as a poisoner of horses.

Sometimes, from the garret window of some hunchbacked house near the water, a woman would dump a bucket of ashes onto the head of a passerby. As he gasped and choked, the Swamp Angels would descend upon him, drag him down the basement steps, and pillage him.

Such were the years of apprenticeship of Bill Harrigan, the future Billy the Kid. He felt no scorn for theatrical fictions: he liked to go to the theater (perhaps with no presentiment that they were the symbols and letters of his own destiny) to see the cowboy shows.

Go West!

If the packed theater houses of the Bowery (whose audiences would yell "H'ist dat rag!" when the curtain failed to rise promptly at the scheduled time) presented so many of those gallop-and-shoot "horse operas," the reason is that America was experiencing a fascination with the West. Beyond the setting sun lay the gold of Nevada and California. Beyond the setting sun lay the cedar-felling ax, the buffalo's huge Babylonian face, Brigham Young's top hat and populous marriage bed, the red man's ceremonies and his wrath, the clear desert air, the wild prairie, the elemental earth whose nearness made the heart beat faster, like the nearness of the sea. The West was beckoning. A constant, rhythmic murmur filled those years: the sound of thousands of Americans settling the West. That procession, in the year 1872, was joined by the always coiled and ready to strike* Bill Harrigan, fleeing a rectangular cell.

A Mexican Felled

History (which, like a certain motion-picture director, tells its story in discontinuous images) now offers us the image of a hazardous bar set in the midst of the all-powerful desert as though in the midst of the sea. The time—one changeable night in the year 1873; the exact place—somewhere on the Llano Estacado, in New Mexico. The land is almost preternaturally flat, but the sky of banked clouds, with tatters of storm and moon, is covered with dry, cracked watering holes and mountains. On the ground, there are a cow skull, the howls and eyes of a coyote in the darkness, fine horses, and the long shaft of light from the bar. Inside, their elbows on the bar, tired, hard-muscled men drink a belligerent alcohol and flash stacks of silver coins marked with a serpent and an eagle. A drunk sings impassively. Some of the men speak a language with many *s*'s—it must be Spanish, since those who speak it are held in contempt by the others. Bill Harrigan, the red-haired tenement house rat, is among the drinkers. He has downed a couple of shots and is debating (perhaps because he's flat broke) whether to call for another. The men of this desert land baffle him. To him they look huge and terrifying, tempestuous, happy, hatefully knowledgeable in their handling of wild cattle and big horses. Suddenly there is absolute silence, ignored only by the tin-eared singing of the drunk. A brawny, powerful-looking giant of a Mexican with the face of an old Indian woman has come into the bar. His enormous sombrero and the two pistols on his belt make him seem even larger than he is. In a harsh English he wishes all the gringo sons of bitches drinking in the place a *buenas noches*. No one takes up the gauntlet. Bill asks who the Mexican is, and someone whispers fearfully that the dago (Diego) is Belisario Villagrán, from Chihuahua. Instantly, a shot rings out. Shielded by the ring of tall men around him, Bill has shot the intruder. The glass falls from Villagrán's hand; then, the entire man follows. There is no need for a second shot. Without another look at the sumptuous dead man, Bill picks up the conversation where he left off.

"Is that so?" he drawled. "Well, I'm Bill Harrigan, from New York."

The drunk, insignificant, keeps singing.

The sequel is not hard to foresee. Bill shakes hands all around and accepts flattery, cheers, and whisky. Someone notices that there are no notches on Billy's gun, and offers to cut one to mark the killing of Villagrán. Billy the Kid keeps that someone's knife, but mutters that "Mexicans ain't worth makin' notches for." But perhaps that is not enough. That night Billy lays his blanket out next to the dead man and sleeps—ostentatiously—until morning.

Killing For The Hell Of It

Out of the happy report of that gunshot (at fourteen years of age) the hero Billy the Kid was born and the shifty Bill Harrigan buried. The scrawny kid of the sewers and skullcracking had risen to the rank of frontiersman. He became a horseman; he learned to sit a horse straight, the way they did in Texas or Wyoming, not leaning back like they did in Oregon and California. He never fully measured up to the legend of himself, but he came closer and closer as time went on. Something of the New York hoodlum lived on in the cowboy; he bestowed upon the Mexicans the hatred once inspired in him by Negroes, but the last words he spoke (a string of curses) were in Spanish. He learned the vagabond art of cattle driving and the other, more difficult art of driving men; both helped him be a good cattle rustler.

Sometimes, the guitars and brothels of Mexico reached out and pulled him in. With the dreadful lucidity of insomnia, he would organize orgies that went on for four days and four nights. Finally, in revulsion, he would pay the bill in bullets. So long as his trigger finger didn't fail him, he was the most feared (and perhaps most empty and most lonely) man on that frontier. Pat Garrett, his friend, the sheriff who finally killed him, once remarked: "I've practiced my aim a good deal killing buffalo." "I've practiced mine more'n you have, killing men," Billy softly replied. The details are lost forever, but we know that he was responsible for as many as twenty-one killings—"not counting Mexicans." For seven daring and dangerous years he indulged himself in that luxury called anger.

On the night of July 25, 1880, Billy the Kid came galloping down the main (or only) street of Fort Sumner on his pinto. The heat was oppressive, and the lamps were not yet lighted; Sheriff Garrett, sitting on the porch in a rocking chair, pulled out his gun and shot Billy in the stomach. The horse went on; the rider toppled into the dirt street. Garrett put a second bullet in him. The town (knowing the wounded man was Billy the Kid) closed and locked its windows. Billy's dying was long and blasphemous. When the sun was high, the townspeople began to approach, and someone took his gun; the man was dead. They noted in him that unimportant sort of look that dead men generally have.

He was shaved, sewn into tailor-made clothes, and exhibited to horror and mockery in the shopwindow of the town's best store.

Men on horses or in gigs came in from miles around. On the third day, they had to put makeup on him. On the fourth, to great jubilation, he was buried.

The Uncivil Teacher of Court Etiquette Kôtsuké no Suké

The iniquitous protagonist of this chapter is the uncivil courtier Kira Kôtsuké no Suké, the fateful personage who brought about the degradation and death of the lord of the castle of Ako yet refused to take his own life, honorably, when fitting vengeance so demanded. He was a man who merits the gratitude of all men, for he awakened priceless loyalties and provided the black yet necessary occasion for an immortal undertaking. A hundred or more novels, scholarly articles, doctoral theses, and operas—not to mention effusions in porcelain, veined lapis lazuli, and lacquer—commemorate the deed. Even that most versatile of media, celluloid, has served to preserve the exploit, for "Chushingura, or The Doctrinal History of the Forty-seven Loyal Retainers" (such is the title of the film) is the most oft-presented inspiration of Japanese filmmaking. The minutely detailed glory which those ardent tributes attest is more than justifiable—it is immediately just, in anyone's view.

I follow the story as told by A. B. Mitford, who omits those continual distractions lent by "local color," preferring instead to focus on the movement of the glorious episode. That admirable lack of "Orientalism" allows one to suspect that he has taken his version directly from the Japanese.

42

The Untied Ribbon

In the now faded spring of 1702, Asano Takumi no Kami, the illustrious lord of the castle of Ako, was obliged to receive an envoy from the emperor and offer the hospitality and entertainment of his home to him. Two thousand three hundred years of courtesy (some mythological) had brought the rituals of reception to a fine point of anguished complication. The ambassador represented the emperor, but did so by way of allusion, or symbolically—and this was a nuance which one emphasized too greatly or too little only at one's peril. In order to avoid errors which might all too easily prove fatal, an official of the court at Yedo was sent beforehand to teach the proper ceremonies to be observed. Far from the comforts of the court, and sentenced to this backwoods *villégiature* (which to him must have seemed more like a banishment than a holiday), Kira Kôtsuké no Suké imparted his instructions most ungraciously. At times the magisterial tone of his voice bordered on the insolent. His student, the lord of the castle of Ako, affected to ignore these affronts; he could find no suitable reply, and discipline forbade the slightest violence. One morning, however, the ribbon on the courtier's sock came untied, and he requested that the lord of the castle of Ako tie it up for him again. This gentleman did so, humbly yet with inward indignation. The uncivil teacher of court etiquette told him that he was truly incorrigible—only an ill-bred country bumpkin was capable of tying a knot as clumsily as that. At these words, the lord of the castle of Ako drew his sword and slashed at the uncivil courtier, who fled—the graceful flourish of a delicate thread of blood upon his forehead. . . .A few days later, the military court handed down its sentence against the attacker: the lord of the castle of Ako was to be allowed to commit *hara kiri.* In the central courtyard of the castle of Ako, a dais was erected and covered in red felt, and to it the condemned man was led; he was given a short knife of gold and gems, he confessed his crime publicly, he allowed his upper garments to slip down to his girdle so that he was naked to the waist, and he cut open his abdomen with the two ritual movements of the dirk. He died like a Samurai; the more distant spectators saw no blood, for the felt was red. A white-haired man of great attention to detail—the councillor Oishi Kuranosuké, his second—decapitated his lord with a saber.

The Feigner of Iniquities

Takumi no Kami's castle was confiscated, his family ruined and eclipsed, his name linked to execration. His retainers became Rônins.* One rumor has it that the same night the lord committed *hara kiri*, forty-seven of these Rônins met on the summit of a mountain, where in minute detail they planned the act that took place one year later. But the fact is that the retainers acted with well-justified delay, and at least one of their confabulations took place not on the difficult peak of a mountain, but in a chapel in a forest, an undistinguished pavilion of white-painted wood, unadorned save for the rectangular box that held a mirror.

The Rônins hungered for revenge, but revenge must have seemed unattainable. Kira Kôtsuké no Suké, the hated teacher of court etiquette, had fortified his house, and a cloud of archers and swordsmen swarmed about his palanquin. Among his retinue were incorruptible, secret spies upon whom no detail was lost, and no man did they so closely spy upon and follow as the councillor Kuranosuké, the presumed leader of the avenging Rônins. But by chance Kuranosuké discovered the surveillance, and he based his plan for vengeance upon that knowledge.

He moved to Kiôto, a city unparalleled throughout the empire for the color of its autumns. He allowed himself to descend into the depths of brothels, gambling dens, and taverns. In spite of the gray hairs of his head, he consorted with prostitutes and poets, and with persons even worse. Once he was expelled from a tavern and woke up to find himself in the street, his head covered with vomit.

It happened that a Satsuma man saw this, and said, sadly yet with anger, "Is not this Oishi Kuranosuké, who was a councillor to Asano Takumi no Kami, and who helped him to die yet not having the heart to avenge his lord, gives himself up to women and wine? Faithless beast! Fool and craven! Unworthy the name of a Samurai!"

And he trod on Kuranosuké's face as he slept, and spat on him. When Kôtsuké no Suké's spies reported this passivity, the courtier felt much relieved.

But things did not stop there. The councillor sent his wife and two younger children away and bought a concubine; this iniquitous act cheered the heart and relaxed the fearful prudence of his enemy, who at last dismissed half his guards.

On one of the bitter nights of the winter of 1703, the forty-seven Rônins met in an unkempt garden on the outskirts of Yedo, near a bridge and the playing card factory. They carried the pennants and banners of their lord. Before they began the assault, they informed the inhabitants of the city that they were not raiding the town but embarking on a military mission of strict justice.

The Scar

Two groups attacked the palace of Kira Kôtsuké no Suké. The councillor Kuranosuké led the first, which assaulted the main gate; the second was led by the councillor's elder son, who was not yet sixteen years old and who died that night. History records the many moments of that extraordinarily lucid nightmare—the perilous, pendular descent of the rope ladders, the drum beating the signal of attack, the defenders' rush to defend, the archers posted on the rooftops, the unswerving path of the arrows toward vital organs, the porcelains dishonored by blood, the burning death that turns to ice—all the brazen and disorderly elements of death. Nine of the Rônins died; the defenders were no less brave, and they would not surrender. Shortly after midnight, all resistance ended.

Kira Kôtsuké no Suké, the ignominious cause of all that loyalty, was nowhere to be found. The attackers sought him through every corner of the emotion-torn palace; they were beginning to despair of finding him, when the councillor noted that his bedclothes were still warm. Again the Rônins searched, and soon they discovered a narrow window, hidden by a bronze mirror. Below, in a gloomy courtyard, a man in white looked up at them; a trembling sword was in his right hand. When they rushed down, the man gave himself up without a fight. His forehead bore a scar—the old rubric left by Takumi no Kami's blade.

Then the bloody Rônins went down on their knees to the detested nobleman and told him that they were the former retainers of the lord of the castle of Ako, for whose death and perdition he was to blame, and they requested that he commit the suicide that befitted a samurai.

In vain did the retainers propose to the lord's servile spirit that act of self-respect. He was a man impervious to the pleas of honor; at sunrise, the officers had to slit his throat.

The Evidence

Their thirst for revenge now quenched (but without wrath, or agitation, or regret), the Rônins made their way toward the temple that sheltered the remains of their lord.

In a brass pail they carried the incredible head of Kira Kôtsuké no Suké, and they took turns watching over it. They crossed fields and provinces, in the honest light of day. Men blessed them and wept. The prince of Sendai offered them his hospitality, but they replied that their lord had been waiting for them for almost two years. At last they reached the dark sepulcher, and they offered up the head of their enemy.

The Supreme Court handed down its verdict, and it was as expected: the retainers were granted the privilege of suicide. All obeyed, some with ardent serenity, and they lie now beside their lord. Today, men and children come to the sepulcher of those faithful men to pray.

The Satsuma Man

Among the pilgrims who come to the grave, there is one dusty, tired young man who must have come from a great distance. He prostrates himself before the monument to the councillor Oishi Kuranosuké and he says aloud: "When I saw you lying drunk by the roadside, at the doorstep of a whorehouse in Kiôto, I knew not that you were plotting to avenge your lord; and, thinking you to be a faithless man, I trampled on you and spat in your face as I passed. I have come to offer atonement." He spoke these words and then committed *hara kiri*.

The priest of the temple where Kuranosuké's body lay was greatly moved by the Satsuma man's courage, and he buried him by the side of the Rônins and their lord.

This is the end of the story of the forty-seven loyal retainers—except that the story has no ending, because we other men, who are perhaps not loyal yet will never entirely lose the hope that we might one day be so, shall continue to honor them with our words.*

Hakim, the Masked Dyer of Merv

For Angélica Ocampo

Unless I am mistaken, the original sources of information on Al-Moqanna, the Veiled (or, more strictly, Masked) Prophet of Khorasan, are but four: (a) the excerpts from the *History of the Caliphs* preserved by Bāladhūrī; (b) the *Manual of the Giant, or Book of Precision and Revision*, by the official historian of the Abbasids, Ibn Abī Tahīr Tarfur; (c) the Arabic codex entitled *The Annihilation of the Rose*, which refutes the abominable heresies of the *Rosa Obscura* or *Rosa Secreta*, which was the Prophet's holy work; and (d) several coins (without portraits) unearthed by an engineer named Andrusov on ground that had been leveled for the Trans-Caspian Railway. These coins were deposited in the Numismatic Museum in Tehran; they contain Persian distichs which summarize or correct certain passages from the *Annihilation*. The original *Rosa* has apparently been lost, since the manuscript found in 1899 and published (not without haste) by the Morgenländisches Archiv was declared by Horn, and later by Sir Percy Sykes, to be apocryphal.

The fame of the Prophet in the West is owed to Thomas Moore's garrulous poem *Lalla Rookh*, a work laden with the Irish conspirator's sighs and longings for the East.

The Scarlet Dye

In the year 120 of the Hegira, or 736 of the Christian era, there was born in Turkestan the man Hakim, whom the people of that time and that region were to call The Veiled. His birthplace was the ancient city of Merv, whose gardens and vineyards and lawns look out sadly onto the desert. Noontime there, when not obscured by choking clouds of sand that leave a film of whitish dust on the black clusters of the grapes, is white and dazzling.

Hakim was raised in that wearied city. We know that one of his father's brothers trained him as a dyer—the craft, known to be a refuge for infidels and impostors and inconstant men, which inspired the first anathemas of his extravagant career. *My face is of gold,* a famous page of the *Annihilation* says, *but I have steeped the purple dye and on the second night have plunged the uncarded wool into it, and on the third night have saturated the prepared wool, and the emperors of the islands still contend for that bloody cloth. Thus did I sin in the years of my youth, deforming the true colors of the creatures. The Angel would tell me that lambs were not the color of tigers, while Satan would say to me that the All-Powerful One desired that they be, and in that pursuit he employed my cunning and my dye. Now I know that neither the Angel nor Satan spoke the truth, for I know that all color is abominable.*

In the year 146 of the Hegira, Hakim disappeared from his native city. The vats and barrels in which he had immersed the cloth were broken, as were a scimitar from Shiraz and a brass mirror.

The Bull

At the end of the moon of Sha'ban in the year 158, the air of the desert was very clear, and a group of men were looking toward the west in expectation of the moon of Ramadan, which inspires fasting and mortification. They were slaves, beggars, horse sellers, camel thieves, and butchers. Sitting gravely on the ground before the gate of an inn at which caravans stopped on the road to Merv, they awaited the sign. They looked at the setting sun, and the color of the setting sun was the color of the sand.

From far out on the dizzying desert (whose sun gives men fever and whose moon brings on convulsions), they saw three figures, apparently of immense height, coming toward them. The three figures were human, but the one in the center possessed the head of a bull. As these figures came closer, the man in the center was seen to be wearing a mask, while the two men that accompanied him were blind.

Someone (as in the tales of the *Thousand and One Nights*) asked the reason for this wonder. *They are blind*, the masked man said, *because they have looked upon my face.*

The Leopard

The historian of the Abbasids relates that the man from the desert (whose voice was extraordinarily sweet, or so, in contrast to the harshness of the mask, it seemed to be) told the men that though they were awaiting the sign of a month of penitence, he would be for them a greater sign: the sign of an entire *life* of penitence, and a calumniated death. He told them that he was Hakim, son of Ozman, and that in the year 146 of the Flight a man had entered his house and after purifying himself and praying had cut his, Hakim's, head off with a scimitar and taken it up to the heavens. Borne in the right hand of this visitor (who was the angel Gabriel), his head had been taken before the Almighty, who had bade him prophesy, entrusting him with words of such antiquity that speaking them burned one's mouth and endowed one with such glorious resplendence that mortal eyes could not bear to look upon it. That was the reason for his mask. When every man on earth professed the new law, the Visage would be unveiled to them, and they would be able to worship it without danger—as the angels did already. His message delivered. Hakim exhorted the men to *jihad*—a holy war—and the martyrdom that accompanied it.

The slaves, beggars, horse sellers, camel thieves, and butchers denied him their belief—one voice cried *sorcerer*; another, *impostor*.

Someone had brought a leopard—perhaps a member of that lithe and bloodthirsty breed trained by Persian huntsmen. At any rate, it broke free of its cage. Save for the masked Prophet and his two acolytes, all the men there trampled one another in their haste to flee. When they returned, the beast was blind. In the presence of those luminous, dead eyes, the men worshiped Hakim and admitted his supernatural estate.

The Veiled Prophet

The official historian of the Abbasids narrates with no great enthusiasm the inroads made by Hakim the Veiled in Khorasan. That province—greatly moved by the misfortune and crucifixion of its most famous leader—embraced with desperate fervor the doctrine offered by the Shining Visage and offered up to him its blood and gold. (Hakim by now had exchanged his harsh mask for a fourfold veil of white silk embroidered with precious stones. Black was the symbolic color of the caliphs of the House of Abbas; Hakim chose the color white—the most distant from it— for his shielding Veil, his banners, and his turbans.) The campaign began well. It is true that in the *Book of Precision* it is the *caliph's* pennants that are victorious everywhere, but since the most frequent result of those victories is the stripping of the generals of their rank and the abandonment of impregnable castles, it is not difficult for the sagacious reader to read between the lines. Toward the end of the moon of Rajab in the year 161, the famous city of

Nishapur opened its iron gates to the Masked One; in early 162, the city of Astarabad did likewise. Hakim's military operations (like those of another, more fortunate Prophet) were limited to his tenor chanting of prayers offered up to the Deity from the hump of a reddish-colored camel in the chaotic heart of battle. Arrows would whistle all around him, yet he was never wounded. He seemed to seek out danger—the night a band of loathsome lepers surrounded his palace, he had them brought to him, he kissed them, and he made them gifts of gold and silver.

The Prophet delegated the wearying details of governing to six or seven adepts. He was a scholar of meditation and of peace—a harem of 114 blind wives attempted to satisfy the needs of his divine body.

Abominable Mirrors

So long as their words do not altogether contravene orthodox belief, confidential friends of God are tolerated by Islam, however indiscreet or threatening to that religion they may be. The Prophet would perhaps not have spurned the advantages of that neglect, but his followers, his victories, and the public wrath of the caliph—whose name was Muhammad al-Mahdi—forced him into heresy. It was that dissent that ruined him, though first it led him to set down the articles of a personal religion (a personal religion that bore the clear influence of gnostic forebears).

In the beginning of Hakim's cosmogony there was a spectral god, a deity as majestically devoid of origins as of name and face. This deity was an immutable god, but its image threw nine shadows; these, condescending to action, endowed and ruled over a first heaven. From that first demiurgic crown there came a second, with its own angels, powers, and thrones, and these in turn founded another, lower heaven, which was the symmetrical duplicate of the first. This second conclave was reproduced in a third, and the third in another, lower conclave, and so on, to the number of 999. The lord of the nethermost heaven—the shadow of shadows of yet other shadows—is He who reigns over us, and His fraction of divinity tends to zero.

The earth we inhabit is an error, an incompetent parody. Mirrors and paternity are abominable because they multiply and affirm it. Revulsion, disgust, is the fundamental virtue, and two rules of conduct (between which the Prophet left men free to choose) lead us to it: abstinence and utter licentiousness—the indulgence of the flesh or the chastening of it.

Hakim's paradise and hell were no less desperate. *To those who deny the Word, to those who deny the Jeweled Veil and the Visage,* runs an imprecation from the *Rosa Secreta, I vow a wondrous Hell, for each person who so denies shall reign over 999 empires of fire, and in each empire shall be 999 mountains of fire, and upon each mountain there shall be 999 towers of fire, and each tower shall have 999 stories of fire, and each story shall have 999 beds of fire, and in each bed shall that person be, and 999 kinds of fire, each with its own face and voice, shall torture that person throughout eternity.* Another passage corroborates this: *Here, in this life, dost thou suffer one body; in death and Retribution, thou shalt have bodies innumerable.* Paradise was less concrete: *It is always night, and there are fountains of stone, and the happiness of that paradise is the special happiness of farewells, of renunciation, and of those who know that they are sleeping.*

The Visage

In the 163rd year of the Hegira, the fifth of the Shining Face, Hakim was surrounded in Sanam by the Caliph's army. Great were the provisions, many the martyrs, and aid from a horde of angels of light was expected at any moment. Such was the pass to which they had come when a terrifying rumor spread through the castle. It was said that as an adulteress within the harem was being strangled by the eunuchs, she had screamed that the third finger was missing from the Prophet's right hand, and that his other fingers had no nails. The rumor spread like fire among the faithful. In broad daylight, standing upon a high terrace, Hakim prayed to his familiar God for victory, or for a sign. Servilely, with their heads bowed (as though they were running against the rain), two captains snatched away the gem-embroidered veil.

First, there came a trembling. The promised face of the Apostle, the face which had journeyed to the heavens, was indeed white, but it was white with the whiteness of leprosy. It was so swollen (or so incredible) that it seemed to be a mask. It had no eyebrows; the lower eyelid of the right eye drooped upon the senile cheek; a dangling cluster of nodular growths was eating away its lips; the flat and inhuman nose resembled that of a lion.

Hakim's voice attempted one final deception: *Thy abominable sins forbid thee to look upon my radiance . . .,* he began.

No one was listening; he was riddled with spears.

Man on Pink Corner*

For Enrique Amorim

Imagine you bringing up Francisco Real that way, out of the clear blue sky, him dead and gone and all. Because I met the man, even if this wa'n't exactly his stomping ground—his was more up in the north, up around Guadalupe Lake and Bateriá. Truth is, I doubt if I crossed paths with the man more than three times, and all three were on a single night—though it's not one I'll be likely ever to forget. It was the night La Lujanera came home to sleep at my place—just like that, just up and came—and the same night Rosendo Juárez left Maldonado* never to return. Of course you probably haven't had the experience you'd need to recognize that particular individual's name, but in his time Rosendo Juárez— the Sticker, they called him—was one of the toughest customers in Villa Santa Rita. He was fierce with a knife, was Rosendo Juárez, as you'd expect with a moniker like that, and he was one of don Nicolás Paredes' men—don Nicolás being one of Morel's men.* He'd come into the cathouse just as dandified as you can imagine, head to foot in black, with his belt buckle and studs and all of silver. Men and dogs, both, had a healthy respect for him, and the whores did too; everybody knew two killings'd been laid to him already. He wore a tall sort of hat with a narrow brim, which sat down like this on a long mane of greasy hair. Rosendo was favored by fortune, as they say, and we boys in the neighborhood would imitate him right down to the way he spit. But then there came a night that showed us Rosendo Juárez's true colors.

It's hard to believe, but the story of that night—a night as

strange as any I've ever lived through—began with an insolent
red-wheeled hack crammed with men, banging and rattling along
those streets of hard-packed clay, past brick kilns and vacant lots.
There was two men in black, strumming guitars and lost in their
own thoughts, and the man on the driver's seat using his whip
on any loose dogs that took a mind to mess with the piebald in
the traces, and one fellow wrapped tight in a poncho riding in
the middle—which was the Yardmaster that everybody always
talked about, and he was spoiling for a fight, spoiling for a kill.
The night was so cool it was like a blessing from heaven; two of
these fellows were riding up on the folded-back cloth top of the
hack—and it was as though the loneliness made that rattletrap a
veritable parade. That was the first event of the many that took
place, but it wa'n't till a while afterward that we found out this part.
Me and my friends, meantime, we'd been over at Julia's place since
early that evening, Julia's place being a big old barracks-like build-
ing made out of sheets of zinc, between the Gauna road and the
Maldonado. It was a place you could pick out from quite a distance
off, on account of the light from a brazen big red light—and on
account of the hullabaloo too. This Julia, although she was a colored
woman, was as reliable and honest as you could ask for, so there
wa'n't ever any lack of musicians, good drinks, and girls that could
dance all night if they was asked to. But this Lujanera I mentioned,
who was Rosendo's woman, she outdid 'em all, and by a good
long ways. La Lujanera's dead now, señor, and I have to admit that
sometimes whole years go by that I don't think about her, but you
ought to have seen her in her time, with those eyes of hers. Seein'
her wouldn't put a man to sleep, and that's for sure.

Rotgut, milongas, women, a *simpático* kind of curse at you from
the mouth of Rosendo Juárez, a slap on the back from him that
you tried to feel was friendly-like—the truth is, I was as happy
as a man could be. I was paired up with a girl that could follow
like she could read my mind; the tango was having its way with
us, whirling us this way and then that and losing us and calling

us back again and finding us. . . .To make a long story short, we boys were dancing, 'most like bein' in a dream, when all of a sudden the music seemed to get louder, and what it was was that you could begin to hear the guitar-strumming of those two fellows I mentioned, mixing in with the music there at Julia's, and coming nearer every minute. Then the gust of wind that had brought it to us changed direction, and I went back to my own body and my partner's, and the conversations of the dance. A good while later, there came a knock at the front door—a big knock and a big voice, too. At that, everybody got still; then a man's chest bumped the swinging doors open and the man himself stepped inside. The man resembled the voice a good deal.

For us, he wa'n't Francisco Real yet, but you couldn't deny he was a tall, muscular sort of man, dressed head to foot in black, with a shawl around his shoulders about the color of a bay horse. I remember his face being Indian-like, unsociable.

One of the swinging doors hit me when it banged open. Like the damn fool I am, I reached out and swung at the fellow with my left hand while with my right I went for the knife I kept sharp and waiting in the armhole of my vest, under my left arm. If we'd've tangled, I wouldn't have lasted long. The man put out his arm—and it was all he had to do—and brushed me aside, like he was brushing away a fly. So there I was—half sprawled there behind the door, with my hand still under my vest, holding on to my useless weapon, while he just kept walking, like nothing had happened, right on into the room. Just kept walking—taller than any of the boys that were stepping aside to make way for him, and acting like we were all invisible. The first row of fellows—pure Eye-talians, an' all eyes—opened out like a fan, and fast. But that wa'n't about to last. In the pack just behind those first fellows, the Englishman was waiting for him, and before that Englishman could feel the stranger's hand on his shoulder, he floored him with a roundhouse he had waitin'—and no sooner had he landed his punch than the party started in for

57

serious. The place was yards and yards deep, but they herded the stranger from one end of it to the other, bumping him and shoving him and whistling and spitting. At first they'd hit him with their fists, but then when they saw that he didn't so much as put up a hand to try to block their punches, they started slapping him— sometimes with their open hands and sometimes just with the harmless fringe on their shawls, like they were makin' fun of him. And also like they were reserving him for Rosendo, who hadn't budged from where he was standing, back against the back wall, and without saying a word. He was taking quick puffs of his cigarette—I will say that—like he already had an inkling of what the rest of us would see clear enough later on. The Yardmaster— straight and bloody, and the wind from that jeering mob behind him—was getting pushed and shoved back to Rosendo. Whistled at, beaten, spit on, as soon as he came face to face with Rosendo, he spoke. He looked at him and he wiped off his face with his arm, and he said this:

"I'm Francisco Real, from up on the Northside. Francisco Real, and they call me the Yardmaster. I've let these poor sons of bitches lift their hands to me because what I'm looking for is a man. There are people out there—I figure they're just talkers, you know—saying there's some guy down here in these boondocks that fancies himself a knife fighter, and a bad 'un—say he's called the Sticker. I'd like to make his acquaintance, so he could show me—me being nobody, you understand—what it means to be a man of courage, a man you can look up to."

He said that, and he never took his eyes off him. Now a sticker for real glinted in his right hand—no doubt he'd had it up his sleeve the whole time. All around, the fellows that had been pushing to get close started backing away, and every one of us was looking at the two of them, and you could have heard a pin drop. Why, even the black gentleman that played the violin, a blind man he was, he had his face turned that way.

Just then I hear movement behind me, and I see that in the

doorway there's standing six or seven men, which would be the Yardmaster's gang, you see. The oldest of them, a weather-beaten, country-looking man with a gray-streaked mustache, steps forward and stands there like he's dazzled by all the women and all the light, and he very respectfully takes his hat off. The others just stood there watching, keeping their eyes open, ready to step in, you see, if somebody wanted to start playing dirty.

Meantime, what was happening with Rosendo—why hadn't he come out slashing at that swaggering son of a bitch? He hadn't said a word yet, hadn't so much as raised his eyes. His cigarette, I don't know whether he spit it out or whether it just fell out of his face. Finally he managed to get a few words out, but so quiet that those of us down at the other end of the room couldn't hear what he was saying. Then Francisco Real called him out again, and again Rosendo refused to rise to the occasion. So at that, the youngest of the strangers—just a kid he was—he whistled. La Lujanera looked at him with hate in her eyes and she started through that crowd with her braid down her back—through that crowd of men and whores—and she walked up to her man and she put her hand to his chest and she pulled out his naked blade and she handed it to him.

"Rosendo, I think you're needing this," she said.

Right up next to the roof there was this long kind of window that looked out over the creek. Rosendo took the knife in his two hands and he seemed to be trying to place it, like he didn't recognize it. Then all of a sudden he reared back and flung that knife straight through the window, out into the Maldonado. I felt a cold chill run down my spine.

"The only reason I don't carve you up for beefsteak is that you make me sick," said the stranger. At that, La Lujanera threw her arms around this Yardmaster's neck, and she looked at him with those eyes of hers, and she said, with anger in her voice:

"Forget that dog—he had us thinking he was a man."

Francisco Real stood there perplexed for a second, and then he put his arms around her like it was going to be forever, and he yelled at the musicians to play something—a tango, a milonga—and then yelled at the rest of us to dance. The milonga ran like a grass fire from one end of the room to the other. Real danced straight-faced, but without any daylight between him and her, now that he could get away with it. They finally came to the door, and he yelled:

"Make ways, boys—she's gettin' sleepy!"

That's what he said, and they walked out cheek to cheek, like in the drunken dizziness of the tango, like they were drowning in that tango.

I ought to be ashamed of myself. I spun around the floor a couple of times with one of the girls and then I just dropped her—on account of the heat and the crowdedness, I told her—and I slunk down along the wall till I got to the door. It was a pretty night—but a pretty night for who? Down at the corner stood that hack, with those two guitars sitting up straight on the seat, like two Christian gentlemen. It galled me to see those guitars left out like that, to realize that those boys thought so little of us that they'd trust us not even to walk off with their cheap guitars. It made me mad to feel like we were a bunch of nobodies. I grabbed the carnation behind my ear and threw it in a mud puddle and then I stood there looking at it, more or less so I wouldn't have to think of anything else. I wished it was already the next day, so I'd have this night behind me. Just then, somebody elbowed me, and it felt almost like a relief. It was Rosendo, slipping through the neighborhood all by himself.

"Seems like you're always in the way, asshole," he muttered as he passed by me—I couldn't say whether to get it off his chest or because he had his mind on something else. He took the direction where it was darkest, down along the Maldonado; I never saw the man again.

I stood there looking at the things I'd been seeing all my life—a sky that went on forever, the creek flowing angry-like down below there, a sleeping horse, the dirt street, the kilns—and I was struck by the thought that I was just another weed growing along those banks, coming up between the soapworts and the bone piles of the tanneries. What was supposed to grow out of trash heaps if it wa'n't us?—We was big talkers, but soft when it came to a fight, all mouth and no backbone. Then I told myself it wa'n't like that—the tougher the neighborhood, the tougher a man necessarily had to be. A trash heap?—The milonga was having itself a ball, there was plenty of racket in the houses, and the wind brought the smell of honeysuckle. The night was pretty, but so what? There were enough stars that you got dizzy lookin' at 'em, one on top of another up there. I struggled, I tell you, to make myself feel like none of what had happened meant anything to me, but Rosendo's turning tail, that stranger's insufferable bullying—it wouldn't let me alone. The tall son of a bitch had even gotten himself a woman for the night out of it. For that night and many more nights besides, I thought to myself, and maybe for all the rest of his nights, because La Lujanera was serious medicine. Lord knows which way they'd gone. But they couldn't be far. Probably at it hammer and tongs right now, in the first ditch they'd come to.

When I finally got back inside, that perfectly pleasant little dance was still going on, like nothing had ever happened.

Making myself as inconspicuous as I could, I peered around through the crowd, and I saw that one and another of our boys had slipped out, but the guys from the Northside were tangoing along with everybody else. There was no elbowing or words or anything; everything was real polite, but everybody was keeping their eyes open. The music was kind of sleepy, and the girls that were dancing with the Northside boys were as meek as mice.

I was expecting something, but not what turned out to happen.

Outside we heard a woman crying, and then a voice that was familiar in a way, but calm, almost *too* calm, as though it didn't belong to a real person, saying to her:

"Go ahead, darlin', go on in," and then some more of the woman's crying. Then the voice seemed to be getting a little desperate.

"Open the door, I said! Open the door, you motherless bitch, open the door!"

At that, the rickety doors swung open and La Lujanera stepped in, alone. She came in kind of looking over her shoulder, like somebody was herding her inside.

"She's got a spirit back there commanding her," said the Englishman.

"A dead man, my friend," said the Yardmaster then. His face was like a drunkard's. He came in, and he took a few unsteady steps into the clearing that we all made for him, like we had before. He stood there tall, and unseeing, and then he toppled like a post. One of the boys that had come with him turned him over on his back and put his poncho under his head for a pillow. The boy's hands came away bloody. That was when we saw that he had a big knife wound in his chest; his blood was pooling up and turnin' black this bright red neckerchief he was wearing, but that I hadn't noticed before because his shawl had covered it. To try to stop the blood, one of the girls brought over some rotgut and scorched rags. He was in no condition to tell us what'd happened, and La Lujanera was looking at him sort of vacant-like, with her arms just hanging down at her sides. Everybody was asking her what happened with their eyes, and finally she managed to find her voice. She said that after she'd gone outside with the Yardmaster there, they went off to a little vacant lot, and just then a stranger appeared and desperately called out the Yardmaster to fight, and he stabbed him, gave him that wound there, and she swore she didn't know who the man was, but it wa'n't Rosendo.

Who was going to believe that?

The man at our feet was dying. My thought was, whoever had fixed his clock, his hand had been pretty steady. But the Yardmaster was tough, you had to give him that. When he came to the door just now, Julia had been brewing up some *mate*, and the *mate* went around the room and came all the way back to me before he was finally dead. "Cover my face," he said, when he knew he couldn't last anymore. His pride was all he had left, and he wa'n't going to let people gawk at the expressions on his face while he lay there dyin'. Somebody put that high-crowned black hat over his face, and he died under it, without a sound. When his chest stopped rising and falling, somebody got up the nerve to uncover him—he had that tired look that dead men get. He was one of the toughest men there was back then, from Batería to the Southside—but no sooner was he dead and his mouth shut for all time, I lost all my hate for him.

"All it takes to die is to be alive," one of the girls back in the crowd said, and then another one said something else, in a pensive sort of way:

"Man thought so highly of himself, and all he's good for now is to draw flies."

At that, the Northsiders all muttered something to each other, real low, and then two of 'em at the same time said it out loud:

"The woman killed 'im."

One of 'em yelled in her face, asking her if it was her that did it, and they all surrounded her. At that I forgot all about being meek and not getting in anybody's way, and I pushed through to her like a shot. I'm such a damn fool, it's a wonder as mad as I was I didn't pull out the little dagger I always carried on me. I could feel almost everybody—not to say everybody—looking at me.

"Look at this woman's hands," I said with a sneer. "Do they look steady enough—does she look like she'd have heart enough—to put a knife in the Yardmaster like that?"

Then I added, cool but tough at the same time:

"Who'd've thought the dear departed, who they say was a man to be reckoned with on his own turf, would've ended up this way, and in a backwater as dead as this is, where nothin' ever happens unless some strangers wander in to give us somethin' to talk about and stay around to get spit on afterward?"

Nobody rose to that bait, either.

Just then through the silence came the sound of riders. It was the police. For one reason or another, everybody there had reason to keep the law out of this, so they decided that the best thing was to move the body down to the creek. You'll recall that long window that the gleam of the knife sailed through? Well, that's the very same way the man in black went. A bunch of them lifted him up and after they'd separated him from all the money and whatnot he had on him, somebody hacked off his finger to get to the ring he wore. Vultures, señor, to pick over a poor defenseless dead man like that, after another, better man has fixed 'im. Then a heave-ho, and that rushing, long-suffering water carried him away. I couldn't say whether they gutted him*—I didn't want to look. The gray-mustached individual never took his eyes off me. La Lujanera took advantage of all the shuffling-about to disappear.

By the time the law came in to have their look around, the dance had a pretty good head of steam up again. The blind man on the violin knew how to play habaneras the likes of which you won't hear anymore. Outside, the day began to want to dawn a little. There was a line of arborvitae posts along the top of a hill, standing there all alone-like, because you couldn't see the thin strands of wire between 'em that early in the morning.

I strolled nice and easy on home to my place, which was about three blocks away. There was a light burning in the window, but then it went out. When I saw that, I can tell you I moved a good bit faster. And then, Borges, for the second time I pulled out that short, sharp-edged knife I always carried here, under my vest, under my left arm, and I gave it another long slow inspection— and it was just like new, all innocent, and there was not the slightest trace of blood on it.

Et cetera

For Néstor Ibarra

A Theologian in Death

I have been told by angels that when Melancthon died, a house was prepared for him like that in which he had lived in the world. This also is done with most of the new-comers, owing to which they do not know that they are not still in the natural world. . . . The things in his room, also, were all like those he had before, a similar table, a similar desk with compartments, and also a similar library; so that as soon as he awakened from sleep, he seated himself at the table and continued his writing, as if he were not a dead body, and this on the subject of justification by faith alone, and so on for several days, and writing nothing whatever concerning charity. As the angels perceived this, he was asked through messengers why he did not write about charity also. He replied that there was nothing of the church in charity, for if that were to be received as in any way an essential attribute of the church, man would also ascribe to himself the merit of justification and consequently of salvation, and so also he would rob faith of its spiritual essence. He said these things arrogantly, but he did not know that he was dead and that the place to which he had been sent was not heaven. When the angels perceived this, they withdrew. . . .

A few weeks after this, the things which he used in his room began to be obscured, and at length to disappear, until at last there was nothing left there but the chair, the table, the paper and the inkstand; and, moreover, the walls of his room seemed to be plastered with lime, and the floor to be covered with a yellow, brick-like material, and he himself seemed to be more coarsely clad. Still, he went on writing, and since he persisted in his denial of charity . . . he suddenly seemed to himself to be under ground in a sort of work-house, where there were other theologians like him. And when he wished to go out he was detained. . . .At this, he began to question his ideas, and he was taken out, and sent back to his former chamber. . . .When sent back, he appeared clad in a hairy skin, but he tried to imagine that what had gone before had been a mere hallucination, and he went on praising faith and denying charity. One evening at dusk, he felt a chill. That led him to walk through the house, and he realized that the other rooms were no longer those of the dwelling in which he had lived on earth. One room was filled with unknown instruments, another had shrunk so much that he could not enter it; another one had not itself changed, but its windows and doors opened onto great sand dunes. There was a room at the rear of the house in which there were three tables, at which sat men like himself, who also cast charity into exile, and he said that he conversed with them, and was confirmed by them day by day, and told that no other theologian was as wise as he. He was smitten by that adoration, but since some of the persons had no face, and others were like dead men, he soon came to abominate and mistrust them. Then he began to write something about charity; but what he wrote on the paper one day, he did not see the next; for this happens to every one there when he commits any thing to paper from the external man only, and not at the same time from the internal, thus from compulsion and not from freedom; it is obliterated of itself. . . .

When any novitiates from the world entered his room to speak with him and to see him, he was ashamed that they should find him in such a sordid place, and so he would summon one of the magical spirits, who by phantasy could produce various becoming shapes, and who then adorned his room with ornaments and with flowered tapestry. . . .But as soon as the visitors were gone, these shapes vanished, and the former lime-plastering and emptiness returned, and sometimes before.

The last word we have of Melancthon is that the wizard and one of the men without a face carried him out to the sand dunes, where he is now a servant to demons.

(From Emanuel Swedenborg, *Arcana Cœlestia*)*

The Chamber of Statues

In the early days, there was a city in the kingdom of the Andalusians where their monarchs lived and its name was Labtayt or Ceuta, or Jaén. In that city, there was a strong tower whose gate (of two portals breadth) was neither for going in nor for coming out, but for keeping closed. And whenever a King died and another King took the Kingship after him, with his own hands, he set a new and strong lock to that gate, till there were four-and-twenty locks upon the tower, according to the number of Kings. After this time, there came to the throne an evil man, who was not of the old royal house, and instead of setting a new lock, he had a mind to open these locks, that he might see what was within the tower. The grandees of his kingdom forbade him this and pressed him to desist and reproved him and blamed him; they hid from him the iron key ring and told him that it was much easier to add a new lock to the gate than to force four-and-twenty, but he persisted, saying, "Needs must this place be opened." Then they offered him all that their hands possessed of monies and treasures and things of price, of flocks, of Christian idols, of gold and silver, if he would but refrain; still, he would not be baulked, and said "There is no help for it but I open this tower." So he pulled off the locks with his right hand (which will now burn through all eternity) and entering, found within the tower figures of Arabs on their horses and camels, habited in turbands hanging down at the ends, with swords in baldrick-belts thrown over their shoulders and bearing long lances in their hands. All these figures were round, as in life, and threw shadows on the ground; a blind man could identify them by touch, and the front hooves of their horses did not touch the ground yet they did not fall, as though the mounts were rearing. These exquisite figures filled the king with great amazement; even more wonderful was the excellent order and silence that one saw in them, for every figure's head was turned to the same side (the west) while not a single voice or clarion was heard. Such was the first room in the castle. In the second, the king found the table that belonged to Suleyman, son of David—salvation be with both of them! This table was carved from a single grass-green emerald, a stone whose occult properties are indescribable yet genuine, for it calms the tempest, preserves the chastity of its wearer, keeps off dysentery and evil spirits, brings favorable outcome to lawsuits, and is of great relief in childbearing.

In the third room, two books were found: one was black and taught the virtues of each metal, each talisman, and each day, together with the preparation of poisons and antidotes; the other was white, and though the script was clear, its lesson could not be deciphered. In the fourth room found he a mappa mundi figuring the earth and the seas and the different cities and countries and villages of the world, each with its true name and exact shape.

In the fifth, they found a marvelous mirror, great and round, of mixed metals, which had been made for Suleyman, son of David—on the twain be forgiveness!—wherein whoso looked might see the counterfeit presentment of his parents and his children, from the first Adam to those who shall hear the Trumpet. The sixth room was filled with that hermetic powder, one drachm of which elixir can change three thousand drachms of silver into three thousand drachms of gold. The seventh appeared empty, and it was so long that the ablest of the king's archers might have loosed an arrow from its doorway without hitting the distant wall. Carved on that far wall, they saw a terrible inscription. The king examined it, and understood it, and it spoke in this wise: "If any hand opens the gate of this castle, the warriors of flesh at the entrance, who resemble warriors of metal, shall take possession of the kingdom."

These things occurred in the eighty-ninth year of the Hegira. Before the year reached its end, Tarik ibn Zayid would conquer that city and slay this King after the sorriest fashion and sack the city and make prisoners of the women and boys therein and get great loot. Thus it was that the Arabs spread all over the cities of Andalusia—a kingdom of fig trees and watered plains in which no man suffered thirst. As for the treasures, it is widely known that Tarik, son of Zayid, sent them to his lord, the caliph Al-Walid bin Abd al-Malik, who entombed them in a pyramid.

(From the *Book of the Thousand Nights and a Night*, Night 272)*

The Story of the Two Dreamers

The Arab historian Al-Ishaqi tells the story of this event:

"It is related by men worthy of belief (though only Allah is omniscient and omnipotent and all-merciful and unsleeping) that a man of Cairo was possessed of ample riches and great wealth; but he was so generous and magnanimous that his wealth passed away, save his father's house, and his state changed, and he became utterly destitute, and could not obtain his sustenance save by laborious exertion. And he slept one night, overwhelmed and oppressed, under a fig tree in his garden, and saw in his sleep a person dripping wet who took from his mouth a golden coin and said to him, 'Verily thy fortune is in Persia, in Isfahan: therefore seek it and repair to it.' So he journeyed to Persia, meeting on the way with all the dangers of the desert, and of ships, and of pirates, and of idolaters, and of rivers, and of wild beasts, and of men; and when he at last arrived there, the evening overtook him, and he slept in a mosque. Now there was, adjacent to the mosque, a house; and as Allah (whose name be exalted!) had decreed, a party of robbers entered the mosque, and thence passed to that house; and the people of the house, awaking at the disturbance occasioned by the robbers, raised cries; the neighbors made a cry as well, whereupon the Wálee came to their aid with his followers, and the robbers fled over the housetops. The Wálee then entered the mosque, and found the man of Cairo sleeping there; so he laid hold upon him, and inflicted upon him a painful beating with mikra'ahs, until he was at the point of death, and imprisoned him; and he remained three days in the prison; after which, the Wálee caused him to be brought, and said to him, 'From what country art thou?' He answered, 'From Cairo.'—'And what affair,' said the Wálee, 'was the cause of thy coming to Persia?' He answered, 'I saw in my sleep a person who said to me, "Verily thy fortune is in Isfahan; therefore repair to it." And when I came here, I found the fortune of which he told me to be those blows of the mikra'ahs, that I have received from thee.'—

"And upon this the Wálee laughed so that his grinders appeared, and said to him, 'O thou of little sense, *I* saw three times in my sleep a person who said to me, "Verily a house in Cairo, in such a district, and of such a description, hath in its court a garden, at the lower end of which is a fountain, wherein is wealth of great amount: therefore repair to it and take it." But I went not; and thou, through the smallness of they sense, hast journeyed from city to city on account of a thing thou hast seen in sleep, when it was only an effect of confused dreams.'—Then he gave him some money, and said to him, 'Help thyself with this to return to thy city.'

"So he took it and returned to Cairo. Now the house which the Wálee had described, in Cairo, was the house of that man; therefore when he arrived at his abode, he dug beneath the fountain, and beheld abundant wealth. Thus God enriched and sustained him; and <u>this was a wonderful coincidence</u>."

(From the *Book of the Thousand Nights and a Night*, Night 351)*

The Wizard that was Made to Wait

In Santiago de Compostela, there was once a dean of the cathedral who was greedy to learn the art of magic. He heard a rumor that a man named Illán, who lived in the city of Toledo, knew more things respecting this art than any other man, and he set off to Toledo to find him.

The day the dean arrived, he went directly to the place where Illán lived and found him at his books, in a room at the rear of the house. Illán greeted the dean kindly, but begged that he put off the business of his journey until after they had eaten. He showed him to a cool apartment and told him he was very glad that he had come. After dinner, the dean explained the purpose of his journey, and asked Illán to teach him the occult science. Illán told him that he had divined that his visitor was a dean, a man of good position and promising future; he told him, also, however, that he feared that should he teach him as he asked, the dean would forget him afterward. The dean promised that he would never forget the kindness shown him by Illán, and said he would be forever in his debt. When that vow was made, Illán told the dean that the magic arts could be learned only in a retired place, and he took him by the hand and led him into an adjoining room, where there was a large iron ring in the floor. First, however, he instructed his serving-woman that they would have partridge for dinner, though he told her not to put them on the fire until he bade her do so. The two men together lifted the iron ring, and they began to descend a stairway hewn with skill from stone; so far did they descend these stairs that the dean would have sworn they had gone beneath the bed of the Tagus. At the foot of the stairway there was a cell, and then a library, and then a sort of cabinet, or private study, filled with instruments of magic. They thumbed through the books, and as they were doing this, two men entered with a letter for the dean. This letter had been sent him by the bishop, his uncle, and it informed him that his uncle was taken very ill; if the dean wished to see him alive, the letter said, he should return home without delay. This news vexed the dean greatly, in the first instance because of his uncle's illness, but second because he was obliged to interrupt his studies. He resolved to send his regrets, and he sent the letter to the bishop. In three days, several men arrived, dressed in mourning and bringing further letters for the dean, informing him that his uncle the bishop had died, that a successor was being chosen, and that it was hoped that by the grace of God he himself would be elected. These letters also said that he should not trouble himself to come, since it would be much better if he were elected *in absentia.*

Ten days later, two very well-turned-out squires came to where the dean was at his studies; they threw themselves at his feet, kissed his hand, and addressed him as "bishop."

When Illán saw these things, he went with great happiness to the new prelate and told him he thanked God that such good news should make its way to his humble house. Then he asked that one of his sons be given the vacant deanship. The bishop informed him that he had reserved that position for his own brother, but that he was indeed resolved to show Illán's son favor, and that the three of them should set off together for Santiago at once.

The three men set off for Santiago, where they were received with great honors. Six months later, the bishop received messengers from the Pope, who offered him the archbishopric of Tolosa and left to the bishop himself the choice of his successor. When Illán learned this news, he reminded the bishop of his old promise and requested the bishopric for his son. The new archbishop informed Illán that he had reserved the bishopric for his own uncle, his father's brother, but that he was indeed resolved to show Illán's son favor, and that they should set off together for Tolosa at once. Illán had no choice but to agree.

The three men set off for Tolosa, where they were received with great honors and with masses. Two years later, the archbishop received messengers from the Pope, who offered him a cardinal's biretta and left to the archbishop himself the choice of his successor. When Illán learned this news, he reminded the archbishop of his old promise and requested the archbishopric for his son. The new cardinal informed Illán that he had reserved the archbishopric for his own uncle, his mother's brother, but that he was indeed resolved to show Illán's son favor, and he insisted that they set out together for Rome at once. Illán had no choice but to agree.

The three men set out together for Rome, where they were received with great honors and with masses and processions. Four years later the Pope died, and our cardinal was unanimously elected to the Holy See by his brother cardinals. When Illán learned this news, he kissed the feet of His Holiness, reminded him of his old promise, and requested that his son be made cardinal in His Holiness' place. The Pope threatened Illán with imprisonment, telling him that he knew very well he was a wizard who when he had lived in Toledo had been no better than a teacher of magic arts. The miserable Illán said he would return to Spain, then, and begged of the Pope a morsel to eat along the way. The Pope refused. Then it was that Illán (whose face had become young again in a most extraordinary way) said in a firm and steady voice:

"Then I shall have to eat those partridges that I ordered up for tonight's supper."

The serving-woman appeared and Illán told her to put the partridges on the fire. At those words, the Pope found himself in the cell under Illán's house in Toledo, a poor dean of the cathedral of Santiago de Compostela, and so ashamed of his ingratitude that he could find no words by which to beg Illán's forgiveness. Illán declared that the trial to which he'd put the dean sufficed; he refused him his portion of the partridges and went with him to the door, where he wished him a pleasant journey and sent him off most courteously.

(From the *Libro de Patronio* by the Infante don
Juan Manuel, who took it in turn from an Arabic
volume, *The Forty Mornings and the Forty Nights*)

The Mirror of Ink

History records that the cruelest of the governors of the Sudan was Yāqub the Afflicted, who abandoned his nation to the iniquities of Egyptian tax collectors and died in a chamber of the palace on the fourteenth day of the moon of Barmajat in the year 1842. There are those who insinuate that the sorcerer Abderramen al-Masmudī (whose name might be translated "The Servant of Mercy") murdered him with a dagger or with poison, but a natural death is more likely—especially as he was known as "the Afflicted." Nonetheless, Capt. Richard Francis Burton spoke with this sorcerer in 1853, and he reported that the sorcerer told him this story that I shall reproduce here:

"It is true that I suffered captivity in the fortress of Yakub the Afflicted, due to the conspiracy forged by my brother Ibrahim, with the vain and perfidious aid of the black chieftains of Kordofan, who betrayed him. My brother perished by the sword upon the bloody pelt of justice, but I threw myself at the abominated feet of the Afflicted One and told him I was a sorcerer, and that if he granted me my life I would show him forms and appearances more marvellous than those of the *fanusi jihal*, the magic lantern. The tyrant demanded an immediate proof; I called for a reed pen, a pair of scissors, a large sheet of Venetian paper, an inkhorn, a chafing-dish with live charcoal in it, a few coriander seeds, and an ounce of benzoin. I cut the paper into six strips and wrote charms and invocations upon the first five; on the last I inscribed the following words from the glorious Qur'ān: 'We have removed from thee thy veil, and thy sight is piercing.' Then I drew a magic square in Yakub's right palm and asked him to hold it out to me; into it, I poured a circle of ink. I asked him whether he could see his face in the circle, and he told me that he could see it clearly. I instructed him not to raise his eyes. I put the benzoin and the coriander seeds into the chafing-dish and therein also burned the invocations. I asked the Afflicted One to name the figure that he wished to see. He thought for a moment and told me that he wished to see a wild horse, the most beautiful creature that grazed upon the meadows that lie along the desert. He looked, and he saw first green and peaceful fields and then a horse coming toward him, as graceful as a leopard and with a white star upon its forehead. He then asked me for a herd of such horses, as perfect as the first, and he saw upon the horizon a long cloud of dust, and then the herd. I sensed that my life was safe.

"Hardly had the sun appeared above the horizon when two soldiers entered my cell and conveyed me to the chamber of the Afflicted One, wherein I found awaiting me the incense, the chafing-dish, and the ink. Thus day by day did he make demands upon my skill, and thus day by day did I show to him the appearances of this world. That dead man whom I abominate held within his hand all that dead men have seen and all that living men see: the cities, climes, and kingdoms into which this world is divided, the hidden treasures of its center, the ships that sail its seas, its instruments of war and music and surgery, its graceful women, its fixed stars and the planets, the colors taken up by the infidel to paint his abominable images, its minerals and plants with the secrets and virtues which they hold, the angels of silver whose nutriment is our praise and justification of the Lord, the passing-out of prizes in its schools, the statues of birds and kings that lie within the heart of its pyramids, the shadow thrown by the bull upon whose shoulders this world is upheld, and by the fish below the bull, the deserts of Allah the Merciful. He beheld things impossible to describe, such as streets illuminated by gaslight and such as the whale that dies when it hears man's voice. Once he commanded me to show him the city men call Europe. I showed him the grandest of its streets and I believe that it was in that rushing flood of men, all dressed in black and many wearing spectacles, that he saw for the first time the Masked One.

"From that time forth, that figure, sometimes in the dress of the Sudanese, sometimes in uniform, but ever with a veil upon its face, crept always into the visions. Though it was never absent, we could not surmise who it might be. And yet the appearances within the mirror of ink, at first momentary or unmoving, became now more complex; they would unhesitatingly obey my commands, and the tyrant could clearly follow them. In these occupations, both of us, it is true, sometimes became exhausted. The abominable nature of the scenes was another cause of weariness; there was nothing but tortures, garrotes, mutilations, the pleasures of the executioner and the cruel man.

"Thus did we come to the morning of the fourteenth day of the moon of Barmajat. The circle of ink had been poured into the palm, the benzoin sprinkled into the chafing-dish, the invocations burned. The two of us were alone. The Afflicted One commanded me to show him a just and irrevocable punishment, for that day his heart craved to see a death. I showed him soldiers with tambours, the stretched hide of a calf, the persons fortunate enough to look on, the executioner with the sword of justice. The Afflicted One marvelled to see this, and said to me: *It is Abu Kir, the man that slew thy brother Ibrahim, the man that will close thy life when I am able to command the knowledge to convoke these figures without thy aid.* He asked me to bring forth the condemned man, yet when he was brought forth the Afflicted One grew still, because it was the enigmatic man that kept the white cloth always before his visage. The Afflicted One commanded me that before the man was killed, his mask should be stripped from him. I threw myself at his feet and said: *O king of time and substance and peerless essence of the century, this figure is not like the others, for we know not his name nor that of his fathers nor that of the city which is his homeland. Therefore, O king, I dare not touch him, for fear of committing a sin for which I shall be held accountable.* The Afflicted One laughed and swore that he himself would bear the responsibility for the sin, if sin it was. He swore this by his sword and by the Qur'ān. Then it was that I commanded that the condemned man be stripped naked and bound to the stretched hide of the calf and his mask removed from him. Those things were accomplished; the horrified eyes of Yakub at last saw the visage—which was his own face. In fear and madness, he hid his eyes. I held in my firm right hand his trembling hand and commanded him to look upon the ceremony of his death. He was possessed by the mirror; he did not even try to turn his eyes aside, or to spill out the ink. When in the vision the sword fell upon the guilty neck, he moaned and cried out in a voice that inspired no pity in me, and fell to the floor, dead.

"Glory to Him Who does not die, and Who holds within His hand the two keys, of infinite Pardon and infinite Punishment."

(From Richard Francis Burton, *The Lake Regions of Equatorial Africa*)*

Mahomed's Double

Since the idea of Mahomed is always connected with religion in the minds of Mahomedans, therefore in the spiritual world some Mahomed or other is always placed in their view. It is not Mahomed himself, who wrote the Koran, but some other who fills his place; nor is it always the same person, but he is changed according to circumstances. A native of Saxony, who was taken prisoner by the Algerines, and turned Mahomedan, once acted in

77

this character. He having been a Christian, was led to speak with them of the Lord Jesus, affirming that he was not the son of Joseph, but the Son of God himself. This Mahomed was afterwards replaced by others. In the place where that representative Mahomed has his station, a fire, like a small torch, appears, in order that he may be distinguished; but it is visible only to Mahomedans.

The real Mahomed, who wrote the Koran, is not at this day to be seen among them. I have been informed that at first he was appointed to preside over them; but being desirous to rule over all the concerns of their religion as a god, he was removed from his station, and was sent down to one on the right side near the south. A certain society of Mahomedans was once instigated by some evil spirits to acknowledge Mahomed as a god, and in order to appease the sedition Mahomed was raised up from the earth or region beneath, and produced to their view; and on this occasion I also saw him. He appeared like corporeal spirits, who have no interior perception. His face was of a hue approaching to black; and I heard him utter these words, "I am your Mahomed," and presently he seemed to sink down again.

(From Emanuel Swedenborg, *Vera Christiana Religio* [1771])*

Index of Sources

The Cruel Redeemer Lazarus Morell
Mark Twain, *Life on the Mississippi*. New York, 1883.
Bernard De Voto, *Mark Twain's America*. Boston, 1932.

The Improbable Impostor Tom Castro
Philip Gosse, *The History of Piracy*. London, Cambridge,
1911.*

The Widow Ching—Pirate
Philip Gosse, *The History of Piracy*. London, Cambridge,
1911.

Monk Eastman, Purveyor of Iniquities
Herbert Asbury, *The Gangs of New York*. New York, 1927.

The Disinterested Killer Bill Harrigan
Frederick Watson, *A Century of Gunmen*. London, 1931.
Walter Noble Burns, *The Saga of Billy the Kid*. New York,
1925.*

The Uncivil Teacher of Court Etiquette Kôtsuké no Suké
A. B. Mitford, *Tales of Old Japan*. London, 1912.

Hakim, the Masked Dyer of Merv
Sir Percy Sykes, *A History of Persia*. London, 1915.
——, *Die Vernichtung der Rose*, nach dem arabischen Urtext
übertragen von Alexander Schulz. Leipzig, 1927.

A Note on the Translation

(from Collected Fictions)

The first known English translation of a work of fiction by the Argentine Jorge Luis Borges appeared in the August 1948 issue of *Ellery Queen's Mystery Magazine*, but although seven or eight more translations appeared in "little magazines" and anthologies during the fifties, and although Borges clearly had his champions in the literary establishment, it was not until 1962, fourteen years after that first appearance, that a book-length collection of fiction appeared in English.

The two volumes of stories that appeared in that *annus mirabilis*—one from Grove Press, edited by Anthony Kerrigan, and the other from New Directions, edited by Donald A. Yates and James E. Irby—caused an impact that was immediate and overwhelming. John Updike, John Barth, Anthony Burgess, and countless other writers and critics have eloquently and emphatically attested to the unsettling yet liberating effect that Jorge Luis Borges' work had on their vision of the way literature was thenceforth to be done. Reading those stories, writers and critics encountered a disturbingly *other* writer (Borges seemed, sometimes, to come from a place even more distant than Argentina, another literary planet), transported into their ken by translations, who took the detective story and turned it into metaphysics, who took fantasy writing and made it, with its questioning and reinventing of everyday reality, central to the craft of fiction. Even as early as 1933, Pierre Drieu La Rochelle, editor of the influential *Nouvelle Revue Française*, returning to France after visiting

Argentina, is famously reported to have said, "*Borges vaut le voyage*"; now, thirty years later, readers didn't have to make the long, hard (though deliciously exotic) journey into Spanish—Borges had been brought to them, and indeed he soon was being paraded through England and the United States like one of those New World indigenes taken back, captives, by Columbus or Sir Walter Raleigh, to captivate the Old World's imagination.

But while for many readers of these translations Borges was a new writer appearing as though out of nowhere, the truth was that by the time we were reading Borges for the first time in English, he had been writing for forty years or more, long enough to have become a self-conscious, self-possessed, and self-*critical* master of the craft.

The reader of the forewords to the fictions will note that Borges is forever commenting on the style of the stories or the entire volume, preparing the reader for what is to come stylistically as well as thematically. More than once he draws our attention to the "plain style" of the pieces, in contrast to his earlier "baroque." And he is right: Borges' prose style is characterized by a determined economy of resources in which every word is weighted, every word (every mark of punctuation) "tells." It is a quiet style, whose effects are achieved not with bombast or pomp, but rather with a single exploding word or phrase, dropped almost as though offhandedly into a quiet sentence: "He examined his wounds and saw, without astonishment, that they had healed." This laconic detail ("without astonishment"), coming at the very beginning of "The Circular Ruins," will probably only at the end of the story be recalled by the reader, who will, retrospectively and somewhat abashedly, see that it changes *everything* in the story; it is quintessential Borges.

Quietness, subtlety, a laconic terseness—these are the marks of Borges' style. It is a style that has often been called intellectual, and indeed it is dense with allusion—to literature, to philosophy, to religion or theology, to myth, to the culture and history of

Buenos Aires and Argentina and the Southern Cone of South America, to the other contexts in which his words may have appeared. But it is also a simple style: Borges' sentences are almost invariably classical in their symmetry, in their balance. Borges likes parallelism, chiasmus, subtle repetitions-with-variations; his only indulgence in "shocking" the reader (an effect he repudiated) may be the "Miltonian displacement of adjectives" to which he alludes in his foreword to *The Maker*.

Another clear mark of Borges' prose is its employment of certain words with, or for, their etymological value. Again, this is an adjectival device, and it is perhaps the technique that is most unsettling to the reader. One of the most famous opening lines in Spanish literature is this: *Nadie lo vio desembarcar en la unánime noche:* "No one saw him slip from the boat in the unanimous night." What an odd adjective, "unanimous." It is so odd, in fact, that other translations have not allowed it. But it is just as odd in Spanish, and it clearly responds to Borges' intention, explicitly expressed in such fictions as "The Immortal," to let the Latin root govern the Spanish (and, by extension, English) usage. There is, for instance, a "splendid" woman: Her red hair glows. If the translator strives for similarity of effect in the translation (as I have), then he or she cannot, I think, avoid using this technique— which is a technique that Borges' beloved Emerson and de Quincey and Sir Thomas Browne also used with great virtuosity.

Borges himself was a translator of some note, and in addition to the translations per se that he left to Spanish culture—a number of German lyrics, Faulkner, Woolf, Whitman, Melville, Carlyle, Swedenborg, and others—he left at least three essays on the act of translation itself. Two of these, I have found, are extraordinarily liberating to the translator. In "Versions of Homer" ("Las versiones homéricas," 1932), Borges makes it unmistakably clear that every translation is a "version"—not *the* translation of Homer (or any other author) but *a* translation, one in a never-ending series, at least an infinite *possible* series. The very idea of *the* (definitive) translation is misguided, Borges tells us; there are only drafts, approximations—*versions*, as he insists on calling them. He chides us: "The concept of 'definitive text' is appealed to only by religion, or by weariness." Borges makes the point even more emphatically in his later essay "The Translators of the 1001 Nights" ("Los traductores de las *1001 Noches*," 1935).

If my count is correct, at least seventeen translators have preceded me in translating one or more of the fictions of Jorge Luis Borges. In most translator's notes, the translator would feel obliged to justify his or her new translation of a classic, to tell the potential reader of this new *version* that the shortcomings and errors of those seventeen or so prior translations have been met and conquered, as though they were enemies. Borges has tried in his essays to teach us, however, that we should not translate "against" our predecessors; a new translation is always justified by the new voice given the old work, by the new life in a new land that the translation confers on it, by the "shock of the new" that both old and new readers will experience from this inevitably new (or renewed) work. What Borges teaches is that we should simply commend the translation to the reader, with the hope that the reader will find in it a literary experience that is rich and moving. I have listened to Borges' advice as I have listened to Borges' fictions, and I—like the translators who have preceded me—have rendered Borges in the style that I hear when I listen to him. I think that the reader of my version will hear something of the genius of his storytelling and his style. For those who wish to read Borges as Borges wrote Borges, there is always *le voyage à l'espagnol*.

The text that the Borges estate specified to be used for this new translation is the three-volume *Obras completas*, published by Emecé Editores in 1989.

In producing this translation, it has not been our intention to produce an annotated or scholarly edition of Borges, but rather a "reader's edition." Thus, bibliographical information (which is often confused or terribly complex even in the most reliable of cases) has not been included except in a couple of clear instances, nor have we taken variants into account in any way; the Borges Foundation is reported to be working on a fully annotated, bibliographically reasoned variorum, and scholars of course can go to the several bibliographies and many other references that now exist. I have, however, tried to provide the Anglophone reader with at least a modicum of the general knowledge of the history, literature, and culture of Argentina and the Southern Cone of South America that a Hispanophone reader of the fictions, growing up in that culture, would inevitably have. To that end, asterisks have been inserted into the text of the fictions, tied to corresponding notes at the back of the book. (The notes often cite sources where interested readers can find further information.)

This volume of stories is purportedly a volume of biographies of reprehensible evildoers; thus we are told by its title. And as biography, the book might be expected to rely greatly upon "sources" of one sort or another; once again, Borges quite consciously (if somewhat deceptively) leads us to expect this, especially with his "Index of Sources" that closes the book. But all that is truer, perhaps, of the book's first incarnation than of its subsequent reprintings, where Borges acknowledges in the Preface (1954) the "fictive" nature of his stories. This is a case, he says, of "changing and distorting (sometimes without aesthetic justification) the stories of other men" to produce a work singularly his own. This *sui generis* documentation—the borrowing and then "doctoring" of other stories, most of which were in English—presents the translator with something of a challenge: to translate Borges even while Borges is cribbing from, translating, and "changing and distorting" other writers' stories. The method I have chosen to employ is to go to the sources that Borges names (and many more besides), to see the ground upon which the changes and distortions were wrought; where Borges is clearly translating phrases, sentences, or even larger pieces of text, I have used the English of the sources, approximating it where necessary to Borges' "editing"—as for example where Borges omits or interpolates a phrase. The New York gangsters in "Monk Eastman," for example, speak as Herbert Asbury quotes them, not specifically as Borges renders them (i.e., translates them from Asbury) into Spanish. The point is, back-translating Borges' translation did not seem to me the most appropriate method to follow in the case when the original source was available and perhaps even known to my intended target audience in English. Thus, likewise, the odd phrasing of some of the English in "The Widow Ching" is another translator's oddness (from the Chinese), or Gosse's, not my own; that is also the case for the Japanese of the other story of Oriental evil. The reader of this volume will especially note this oddness in the excerpts in the section called "Et cetera," where I have allowed the original writer (when in English) or the English-language text (when a translation) to speak in its own tongue; Swedenborg will, I think, be found to have a "peculiar" style.

Following this same logic, where Borges summarizes or simply "writes," I have attempted to translate him without incorporation of the wording of his sources, as he has more than "made a source his own," he has created. Except in rare instances (several ellipses in "Melancthon" and one and another place), I have not wanted to indicate any clear dividing line between the "documentary" and the "imaginary"; nor have I wanted to burden the text with editorial apparatus. I have only sometimes, certainly not always, indicated page numbers or other references for JLB's quotations in the notes or in the text at the place where the quoting occurs, and then where the text is relatively set off to itself and long. The mention of the books within the notes demonstrates, I hope, that good faith of my borrowings. Nor have I made any attempt, either in the text or in the notes, to "correct" Borges; he has changed names (or the spellings of "real" names), dates, numbers, locations, etc., as his literary vision led him to, but the tracing of those "deviations" is a matter which the editors and I have decided should be left to critics and scholarly publications.

More often than one would imagine, Borges' characters are murderers, knife fighters, throat slitters, liars, evil or casually violent men and women—and of course many of them "live" in a time different from our own. They sometimes use language that is strong, and that today may well be offensive—words denoting membership in ethnic and racial groups, for example. In the Hispanic culture, however, some of these expressions can be, and often are, used as terms of endearment—*negro / negra* and *chino / china* come at once to mind. (I am not claiming that Argentina is free of bigotry; Borges chronicles that, too.) All this is to explain a decision as to my translation of certain terms—specifically *rusito* (literally "little Russian," but with the force of "Jew," "sheeny"), *pardo / parda* (literally "dark mulatto," "black-skinned"), and *gringo* (meaning Italian immigrants: "wops," etc.)—that Borges uses in his fictions. I have chosen to use the word "sheeny" for *rusito* and the word "wop" for *gringo* because in the stories in which these words appear, there is an intention to be offensive— a *character's* intention, not Borges'. I have also chosen to use the word "nigger" for *pardo / parda*. This decision is taken not without considerable soul-searching, but I feel there is historical justification for it. In the May 20, 1996, edition of *The New Yorker* magazine, p. 63, the respected historian and cultural critic Jonathan Raban noted the existence of a nineteenth-century "Nigger Bob's saloon," where, out on the Western frontier, husbands would await the arrival of the train bringing their wives from the East. Thus, when a character in one of Borges' stories says, "I knew I could count on you, old nigger," one can almost hear the slight tenderness, or respect, in the voice, even if, at the same time, one winces. In my view, it is not the translator's place to (as Borges put it) "soften or mitigate" these words. Therefore,

I have translated the epithets with the words I believe would have been used in English—in the United States, say—at the time the stories take place.

The footnotes that appear throughout the text of the stories in the *Collected Fictions* are Borges' own, even when they say "Ed."

This translation commemorates the centenary of Borges' birth in 1899; I wish it also to mark the fiftieth anniversary of the first appearance of Borges in English, in 1948. It is to all translators, then, Borges included, that this translation is—unanimously—dedicated.

Andrew Hurley
San Juan, Puerto Rico
June 1998

Acknowledgments

(from Collected Fictions)

I am indebted to the University of Puerto Rico at Río Piedras for a sabbatical leave that enabled me to begin this project. My thanks to the administration, and to the College of Humanities and the Department of English, for their constant support of my work not only on this project but throughout my twenty-odd years at UPR.

The University of Texas at Austin, Department of Spanish and Portuguese, and its director, Madeline Sutherland-Maier, were most gracious in welcoming the stranger among them. The department sponsored me as a Visiting Scholar with access to all the libraries at UT during my three years in Austin, where most of this translation was produced. My sincerest gratitude is also owed those libraries and their staffs, especially the Perry-Castañeda, the Benson Latin American Collection, and the Humanities Research Center (HRC). Most of the staff, I must abashedly confess, were nameless to me, but one person, Cathy Henderson, has been especially important, as the manuscripts for this project have been incorporated into the Translator Archives in the HRC.

For many reasons this project has been more than usually complex. At Viking Penguin, my editors, Kathryn Court and Michael Millman, have been steadfast, stalwart, and (probably more often than they would have liked) inspired in seeing it through. One could not possibly have had more supportive colleagues, or co-conspirators who stuck by one with any greater solidarity.

Many, many people have given me advice, answered questions,

and offered support of all kinds—they know who they are, and will forgive me, I know, for not mentioning them all personally; I have been asked to keep these acknowledgments brief. But two people, Carter Wheelock and Margaret Sayers Peden, have contributed in an especially important and intimate way, and my gratitude to them cannot go unexpressed here. Carter Wheelock read word by word through an "early-final" draft of the translation, comparing it against the Spanish for omissions, misperceptions and mistranslations, and errors of fact. This translation is the cleaner and more honest for his efforts. Margaret Sayers Peden (a.k.a. Petch), one of the finest translators from Spanish working in the world today, was engaged by the publisher to be an outside editor for this volume. Petch read through the late stages of the translation, comparing it with the Spanish, suggesting changes that ranged from punctuation to "readings." Translators want to translate, *love* to translate; for a translator at the height of her powers to read a translation in this painstaking way and yet, while suggesting changes and improvements, to respect the other translator's work, his approach, his thought processes and creativity—even to applaud the other translator's (very) occasional strokes of brilliance—is to engage in an act of selflessness that is almost superhuman. She made the usual somewhat tedious editing process a joy.

I would never invoke Carter Wheelock's and Petch Peden's readings of the manuscripts of this translation—or those of Michael Millman and the other readers at Viking Penguin—as giving it any authority or credentials or infallibility beyond its fair deserts, but I must say that those readings have given me a security in this translation that I almost surely would not have felt so strongly without them. I am deeply and humbly indebted.

First, last, always, and in number of words inversely proportional to my gratitude—I thank my wife, Isabel Garayta.

Andrew Hurley
San Juan, Puerto Rico
June 1998

Notes to the Fictions

(from Collected Fictions)

These notes are intended only to supply information that a Latin American (and especially Argentine or Uruguayan) reader would have and that would color or determine his or her reading of the stories. Generally, therefore, the notes cover only Argentine history and culture; I have presumed the reader to possess more or less the range of general or world history or culture that JLB makes constant reference to, or to have access to such reference books and other sources as would supply any need there. There is no intention here to produce an "annotated Borges," but rather only to illuminate certain passages that might remain obscure, or even be misunderstood, without that information.

For these notes, I am deeply indebted to *A Dictionary of Borges* by Evelyn Fishburn and Psiche Hughes (London: Duckworth, 1990). Other dictionaries, encyclopedias, reference books, biographies, and works of criticism have been consulted, but none has been as thorough and immediately useful as the *Dictionary of Borges*. In many places, and especially where I quote Fishburn and Hughes directly, I cite their contribution, but I have often paraphrased them without direct attribution; I would not want anyone to think, however, that I am unaware or unappreciative of the use I have made of them. Any errors are my own responsibility, of course, and should not be taken to reflect on them or their work in any way. Another book that has been invaluable is Emir Rodríguez Monegal's *Jorge Luis Borges: A Literary Biography* (New York: Paragon Press, [paper] 1988), now out of print. In the notes, I have cited this work as "Rodríguez Monegal, p. x."

The names of Arab and Persian figures that appear in the stories are taken, in the case of historical persons, from the English transliterations of Philip K. Hitti in his work *History of the Arabs from the Earliest Times to the Present* (New York: Macmillan, 1951). (JLB himself cites Hitti as an authority in this field.) In the case of fictional characters, the translator has used the system of transliteration implicit in Hitti's historical names in comparison with the same names in Spanish transliteration.— *Translator.*

A Universal History of Iniquity

For the peculiarities of the text of the fictions in this volume, the reader is referred to A Note on the Translation.

Preface to the First Edition

p. 3: *Evaristo Carriego:* Carriego (1883–1912) was in fact a popular poet and playwright, and the "particular biography" was the one Borges himself wrote of him (published 1930). Carriego was only a mediocre poet, perhaps, and he left but a single volume (*Misas herejes,* "Heretical Masses") upon his early death from tuberculosis, but his ties to "old Buenos Aires," and especially to the lower-class (and mostly Italian) suburb of Palermo, made him an important figure for Borges. While it is probably exaggerated to say that much of JLB's fascination with the *compadre* (see the note to the title of "Man on Pink Corner" below) and the knife fights and tangos that are associated with that "type" can be traced to Carriego, there is no doubt that as an example of the literary possibilities to which such subject matter can be put, Carriego was very important to JLB and JLB's imagination. Carriego was also the first *professional* writer Borges had ever run across, a man who made his living at writing, and not some "mere" amateur; he held out therefore the possibilities of a true literary career to match Borges's clear literary calling.

Preface to the 1954 Edition

p. 4: *Baltasar Gracián:* Gracián (1601–1658) was a Jesuit priest and a writer (and sometime æsthetician) of the baroque. His name is associated with a treatise called *Agudeza y arte de ingenio* ("Keenness of Mind and the Art of Wit"), and with the Spanish baroque poets Francisco Quevedo and Luis de Góngora.

The Cruel Redeemer Lazarus Morell

p. 7: Pedro Figari: Figari (1861–1938) was a Uruguayan painter "who used fauvist techniques [Rodríguez Monegal, p. 194]" (this perhaps explains his success in Paris, where he lived from 1925 to 1933) and who spent an important part of his life in Buenos Aires (1921–1925). Borges knew the painter rather well and wrote an introduction to a book on him; Figari was also feted by the literary group associated with the review *Martín Fierro*, of which Borges was an important member. His work "was inspired by the life of Negroes and gauchos" (*Oeuvres complètes*, vol. I, ed. Jean Pierre Bernès [Paris: Gallimard, p. 1489].

p. 7: Vicente Rossi: Rossi (1871–1945) was the author of a volume titled *Cosas de negros* ("Negro Matters" [1926]), to which this mention surely points, but he also produced the first reference book on the birth and development of Argentine theater and an important book on the gaucho. He was, then, something of a folklorist and literary historian. In *Evaristo Carriego*, Borges calls Rossi "our best writer of combat prose."

p. 7: Antonio ("Falucho") Ruiz: "Falucho" (d. 1824) was a black Argentine soldier who fought in the wars of independence. His statue once stood near that of General San Martín near the center of Buenos Aires.

p. 7: The stout bayonet charge of the regiment of "Blacks and Tans" . . . against that famous hill near Montevideo: On the last day of 1812 a troop of soldiers made up of Negroes and mulattoes (the reference to the English military group organized to fight the Irish independence uprising is the translator's, but it is almost inevitable, and the irony of the situation would not be lost on Borges; see the story "Theme of the Hero and Traitor" in *Fictions*), under the leadership of the Argentine general Miguel Estanislao Soler, defeated the Spanish troops at the Cerrito, a prominent hill overlooking Montevideo.

p. 7: Lazarus Morell: This particular rogue's true name seems to have been John A. Murrell (Bernard De Voto, *Mark Twain's America* [Boston: Little, Brown, 1932], pp. 16–17 et seq.) or Murell (Mark Twain, *Life on the Mississippi*, intro. James M. Cox [New York: Penguin, 1984 (orig. publ. in United States by James R. Osgood in 1883)].) Interestingly, Twain never gives the rogue's first name; it is possible, then, that JLB, needing a name, took "Lazarus" to fit the ironic notion that Morell gave a second life to the slaves he freed.

pp. 14–15: "I walked four days ... my course for Natchez": Here
Borges is quoting/translating fairly directly from Twain's *Life on the
Mississippi,* pp. 214–215 (Penguin ed. cited in the note just above).
Throughout this story, JLB inserts a phrase here, a sentence there from
Twain, but then, when he says he is quoting, as in the case of the
preaching and horse thieving, he is in reality inventing the quotation
and imagining a scene that Twain only suggests.

The Widow Ching—Pirate

p. 24: Axia's rebuke to Boabdil: Boabdil is Abu 'Abd Allah (Muhammad XII), the last Moorish king of Granada (r. 1482–1492); Aixa was
his mother. The reproof that supposedly was given Boabdil by Aixa
upon the Moors' defeat and expulsion from what had been Islamic Spain
is substantially as Borges reports it here, and the words here given Anne
Bonney are substantially those given in Gosse's *History of Piracy,* p. 203.
(See the "Index of Sources" p. 64.)

p. 25: Rules for pirates: These may actually be found, as quoted, but
in a different order, in Gosse's *History of Piracy,* p. 272. (See "Index of
Sources," p. 64, for bibliographical information.)

p. 29: Quotation on peace in the waters of China: Gosse, p. 278. Note
also that the widow's new name, while indeed given in Gosse, is
attributed to another personage who learned a lesson from the emperor.
This is but one of countless examples of the way JLB changes things,
even dates, to fit his purposes, purposes that one must confess sometimes
are enigmatic. Why change the date of Tom Castro's being found guilty
from February 26 to February 27? Monk Eastman's death from December
26 to December 25? The spelling of Morell/Murrell/Murell's name?
Here the theory of translation must needs be a theory of artistic creativity.

Monk Eastman, Purveyor of Iniquities

p. 30: Resigned: Borges uses this curious word, which I have not
wanted to "interpret," apparently to indicate the fatedness, or ritual
aspect, of this duel. It is as though the word indicated "resigned to fate."
This aspect of violence, of duels, can be seen throughout Borges; I
would especially refer the reader to the story titled "The Encounter," in
the volume *Brodie's Report,* p. 364.

p. 34: Junín: Site of a famous battle in the wars of independence.

The Battle of Junín took place in the then department of Peru; on August 6, 1824, a cavalry engagement was fought between Simón Bolivar's nationalist forces and the royalist forces under José de Canterac. The tide was turning against the independence forces until the royalist rear was attacked by a force of Peruvian hussars under the command of Isidoro Suárez—one of JLB's forebears and a man who in varying degrees and under varying permutations lends his name to JLB's fictions. The royalists were routed.

p. 36: The Death of Monk Eastman: This story is taken, as JLB indicates, from Asbury's *The Gangs of New York*, generally pp. 274–298, but also, for the quotation about "nicks in his stick," p. xviii. Where JLB has clearly borrowed directly from Asbury and it has been possible to use Asbury's words, I have done so; in other cases, I have just borrowed the appropriate terminology, such as the "Mikado tuck-ups" and the "stuss" games.

The Disinterested Killer Bill Harrigan

p. 38: Always coiled and ready to strike: One of the sources that JLB gives for this story is Frederick Watson's *A Century of Gunmen*, though the truth is, there is not much there that JLB seems actually to have used. With, that is, the possible exception of this phrase, *siempre aculebrado* in the Spanish, which I have rendered conjecturally in this way. *"Aculebrado,"* from the Spanish *culebra*, "snake," calls to mind in the native Spanish speaker the notion of "coiled, like a snake" and also of "snake-like, slithering." On page 77 of his book, Watson quotes an old western novel, which says this: "It's not the custom to war without fresh offence, openly given. You must not smile and shoot. You must not shoot an unarmed man, and you must not shoot an unwarned man. . . .The rattlesnake's code, to warn before he strikes, no better, [i.e., there's no better extant code for a man of the West]: a queer, lop-sided, topsy-turvy, jumbled and senseless code—but a code for all that." Thus it seems that JLB may have wanted to paint Billy the Kid as an even worse "varmint" than the rattlesnake, since the rattlesnake at least gives fair warning, unlike Billy, who, as we see in a moment, shoots the Mexican Villagrán before Villagrán knows what's happening. Perhaps, in fact, that was what made Billy the Kid so dangerous—so dangerous that his *friend* Pat Garrett shot him in cold blood. But whatever JLB's motivation for this word, it is a very mysterious one to use here, however related to all the other animal imagery used throughout this volume.

The Uncivil Teacher of Court Etiquette Kôtsuké no Suké

p. 44: Rônins: In A. B. Mitford's *Tales of Old Japan*, which is the source of much of this story, Mitford inevitably uses this word for the "loyal retainers" of the dead nobleman. The word "Rônin" means literally a "wave-man," one who is tossed about hither and thither, as a wave of the sea. It is used "to designate persons of gentle blood, entitled to bear arms, who, having become separated from their feudal lords [or in this case, of course, vice versa], wander about the country in the capacity of knights-errant. Some went into trade, and became simple wardsmen" (Mitford). While Borges himself does not use this word, the word is inevitably used in English reports of the phenomenon, and so I have thought it appropriate to translate what the Spanish has as "retainers," "captains," etc., by the technical word.

It is possible, of course, that JLB is doing with the Chinese system of loyalties what he did to the world's architecture: remaking it in the likeness of Argentina's. One notes that virtually all the houses that JLB uses in his fictions have long, narrow entrances and interior patios, the very floor plan of the Buenos Aires house of the end of the nineteenth century. Likewise, one senses that JLB may have used the word "captains" in the story to indicate the sort of relationship between the lord and his retainers that was common in the Argentina of caudillos and *their* captains. Thus I recognize that if JLB was trying, consciously or not, to produce this effect, it may be somewhat risky to go all the way to the source, to "Rônin," for the "translation." The reader is notified. Likewise, "Chushingura" is the name by which the dramas, poems, and films are inevitably known in English, so I have incorporated that inevitable cultural reference. From its absence in the Spanish text, one supposes that in Spanish the word "Chushingura" was not used.

p. 47: The source for this story: Much of this story is indeed taken from Mitford's *Tales of Old Japan*, pp. 3–19. I have taken the spelling of the characters' names and several quotations, such as the Satsuma man's, from there.

Man on Pink Corner

p. 55: Title: The title of this story in Spanish is "Hombre de la esquina rosada"; it presents many intriguing possibilities, and therefore many problems, to the translator, not so much for the words as for the cultural assumptions underlying them. This story is in a way a portrait of the *compadrito* (the tough guy of the slums) or the *cuchillero* (knife fighter) and his life; as such, many items of that "local color" that Borges deplored in, for example, stories of the "exotic" Orient are found, though casually and unemphatically presented. The first thing that must be dealt with is perhaps that "pink corner." *Esquina* ("corner") is both the actual street corner (as other translations of this story have given it, without the colorful adjective) and the neighborhood general-store-and-bar, generally located on corners, which was the hangout for the lowlife of the barrio. The reader can see this establishment clearly in "Unworthy" (in the volume titled *Brodie's Report*) and more fleetingly in many other stories. What of the adjective "pink" (*rosada*) then? The Buenos Aires of JLB's memory and imagination still had high, thick stucco or plastered brick walls lining the streets, such as the reader may see in the colonial cities of the Caribbean and Central and South America even today: Havana, San Juan, Santo Domingo in the Dominican Republic, etc. Those walls in Buenos Aires were painted generally bright pastel colors; Borges refers to "sky blue" walls more even than to pink ones. Thus Borges was able to evoke in two words (*esquina rosada*) an old neighborhood of Buenos Aires, populated by toughs and knife fighters, and characterized by bars and bordellos in which that "scandalous" dance the tango was danced. (In its beginnings, the tango was so scandalous that no respectable woman would dance it, and one would see two men—*compadritos*—dancing together on street corners; nor would the tenement houses, which had moved into the large old houses vacated by the higher classes, allow such goings-on, even though these *conventillos,* as they were called, might be none too "respectable"—certainly none too "genteel"—themselves.) In evoking that old Buenos Aires, Borges also evoked "the man"—here, the Yardmaster, Rosendo Juárez, and the nameless narrator of the story, all of whom participate in the coldly violent *ethos* of the *orillero,* the (to us, today) exaggeratedly macho slum dweller (especially along the banks of the Maldonado [see note below]) who defended his honor against even the most imagined slight.

97

However, certain aspects of this "man" will probably strike the non-Argentine reader as curious—for example, those "boots with high-stacked heels" (in the original Spanish, "women's shoes") and that "red carnation" in the first paragraph of the story "Monk Eastman, Purveyor of Iniquities," the same sort of carnation that appears in this story. There is also the shawl worn by the gaucholike Yardmaster. These elements, however, were authentic "touches"; the *compadrito* affected these appearances. Previous translations have apparently tried to give all this "information" by calling the story "Street-corner Man," emphasizing the "tough guy hanging out on the corner" aspect of the story, and one can be sympathetic to that solution. Another intriguing possibility, however, is suggested by Bernès in the first volume of the Gallimard edition of JLB's *Oeuvres complètes*. I translate the relevant paragraph "The title of the original publication, which omits the definite article, reminds the reader of the title of a painting given in the catalog of an art exhibit. It stresses the graphic aspect of the scene, which Borges, in the preface to the 1935 edition, called the 'pictorial intention' of his work. One should think of some title of a piece by Pedro Figari....[p. 1497]" This "impressionist" title, then, should perhaps be retained; what one loses in "information" one gains in suggestion.

p. 55: Maldonado: The Maldonado was a creek that at the time of this story (and many of JLB's other stories) marked the northern boundary of the city of Buenos Aires. The neighborhood around this area was called Palermo, or also Maldonado. This story evokes its atmosphere at one period (perhaps partly legendary); the Maldonado (barrio) was a rough place, and the creek was terribly polluted by the tanneries along its banks.

p. 55: Don Nicolás Paredes ... Morel: Paredes was a famous knife fighter and ward boss for the conservative party in Palermo; Morel was another famed political boss, or caudillo.

p. 64: I couldn't say whether they gutted him: Here and elsewhere in Borges (one thinks, of course, especially of the story titled "The Story from Rosendo Juárez" in the volume *Brodie's Report* and the story in this volume titled "The Cruel Redeemer Lazarus Morell"), a corpse is gutted, or somebody thinks about gutting it. This, according to folk wisdom, is to keep the body from floating up and revealing the murder before the culprit has had good time to get away. Apparently a gutted body did not produce as much gas, or the gas (obviously) would not be contained in an inner cavity. Thus there is an unacknowledged "piece of information" here that the ruffians of the Maldonado and other such neighborhoods tacitly shared—tacitly because it was so obvious that no one needed to spell it out.

Et cetera

A Theologian in Death

p. 67: Attribution: The Swedenborg Concordance: A Complete Work of Reference to the Theological Writings of Emanuel Swedenborg, based on the original Latin writings of the author, compiled, edited, and translated by the Rev. John Faulkner Potts, B.A., 4 vols. (London: Swedenborg Society, 1888). The text quoted here appears in the index (p. 622 of the appropriate volume) under "Melancthon" and is a mixture of the entries indicating two different Swedenborg texts: *A Continuation of the Last Judgment* and *The True Christian Religion.* The reader may find the text under "C.J. 47" and "T.797, 1–4." The full entry on Melancthon in the Concordance runs to p. 624.

The Chamber of Statues

p. 69: Attribution: Freely taken from Sir Richard Burton's *Book of the Thousand Nights and a Night* (New York: Heritage Press, 1934 [1962]), pp. 1319–1321. The reader is referred to A Note on the Translation for more detailed comment on JLB's and the translator's uses of translations.

The Story of the Two Dreamers

p. 71: Attribution: This is freely adapted from a different version of the *1001 Nights,* Edward William Lane's *The Arabian Nights Entertainments*—or *The Thousand and One Nights* (New York: Tudor Publ., 1927), p. 1156. There are several other editions of this work, so the reader may find the tale in another place; Lane does not divide his book quite in the way JLB indicates.

The Mirror of Ink

p. 77: Attribution: One would not want to spoil JLB's little joke, if joke it is, but others before me have pointed out the discrepancy between this attribution and the fact. This story appears nowhere in Burton's *Lake Regions* and only sketchily in the volume that di Giovanni and many others give as the source: Edward William Lane's *Manners dnd Customs of the Modern Egyptians* (1837). Nonetheless, where Borges does seem to be translating (or calquing) the words of the last-named book, I have incorporated Lane's wording and word choices.

Mahomed's Double

p. 78: Attribution: Emanuel Swedenborg, *The True Christian Religion, containing the Universal Theology of the New Church, foretold by the Lord in Daniel VII, 13, 14, and in the Apocalypse XXI, 1, 2,* translated from the Latin of ES (New York: American Swedenborg Printing and Publishing Society, 1886), pp. 531, 829–830.

Index of Sources

p. 79: Source for "The Improbable Impostor Tom Castro": The source given by Borges here is the Philip Gosse book *The History of Piracy;* as one can clearly see, it is the same source cited for "The Widow Ching— Pirate," just below it. In my view, this attribution is the result of an initial error seized upon by Borges for another of his "plays with sources"; as he subsequently admitted freely, and as many critics have noted, much of this story comes from the *Encyclopædia Britannica,* Eleventh Edition, in the article titled "Tichborne Claimant." Here again, where JLB is clearly translating or calquing that source, I have followed it without slavish "transliteration" of JLB's Spanish.

p. 79: Source for "The Disinterested Killer Bill Harrigan": Neither the Walter Noble Burns book nor the Frederick Watson book contains anything remotely approaching the story given by Borges here. Some details are "correct" (if that is the word), such as Billy's long and blasphemous dying, spewing Spanish curses, but little in the larger pattern of the "biography" seems to conform to "life." While Borges claimed in the "Autobiographical Essay" (written with Norman Thomas di Giovanni and published in *The Aleph and Other Stories* [1970]) that he was "in flagrant contradiction" of his "chosen authorit[ies]," the truth is that he followed the authorities fairly closely for all the characters herein portrayed *except* that of Billy the Kid. He did, of course, "change and distort" the stories to suit his own purposes, but none is so cut from whole cloth as that of this gunfighter of the Wild West. The lesson in the "Autobiographical Essay" is perhaps that JLB's predilection for the red herring was lifelong.

BORGES AS TRANSLATOR

IDENTITY
(MIRRORS)

$\neq$ $=$ $=$

$\neq$ $\simeq$ $=$

$\neq$ $=$ $\simeq$

IDENTITY
(MASKS)

TRUTH > LIES < TRUTH

F A I T H

LABIRYNTHS

DESTINY / RANDOMNESS

subjective

relative REALITY indifferent
≠ = =

LIFE IS $\boxed{?}$ AND THEN YOU DIE
↑

Telling & interpreting
stories